Mama's Bible

Mildred Colvin

Historical Christian Romance

Mama's Bible

Copyright©2012 by Mildred Colvin

All Rights Reserved

Cover Photo ©Mildred Colvin

ISBN: 1477511520
ISBN-13: 978-1477511527

Jason released her elbow and stepped back.
He folded his arms and glared at her.

"What was that all about?"

His belligerent stance stirred her anger, giving her the strength she needed to confront him. She folded her arms and lifted her chin. "What? Me staying?"

"You saying you're tired of being ignored."

Katie tossed her head. "Well, you should know."

Jason threw his hands out in a helpless gesture and shook his head. "I always heard women were impossible to understand. Now I believe it."

"Women are? You're the one who's been ignoring me."

"I'm not ignoring you." Jason's voice rose. "I'm looking at you. I'm talking to you. Where could you get the idea I'm ignoring you?"

"What you're doing is yelling at me." Katie's voice rose, too. When Tommy and Rachel straightened and stared at them, she lowered her voice. "But even this is better than pretending I don't exist."

She fought the hurt and tears that wanted to come to the surface. She refused to cry. Instead, she met Jason's frown with determination. "I've scarcely seen you since the night Tommy asked me to give my testimony. Since then, I don't think you've said more than two words to me."

Jason's frown deepened, and he looked away. "Yeah, well I didn't figure you wanted me bothering you."

"And you say women are hard to understand."

DEDICATION

To Becka, the sweetest daughter a mother could have.
I love you!

Chapter 1

Missouri, Spring 1850

*K*atie Donovan's heart pounded in rhythm with the sound of hoof beats on the road behind her. She crawled to the back of the covered wagon and looked out into the moonlit night.

Dark forms took shape in a billow of dust, quickly becoming recognizable as two men on horseback racing toward her and her family. Was it the law? The wagon couldn't outrun horses.

"Dad." Her voice choked. Her hands shook at she touched her neck. Could he hear the hoof beats? She turned and tried again, louder this time. "Dad."

His hand closed around the pistol he had hidden behind the seat.

The breath she sucked in caught in her throat. What had happened to her gentle Irish father? Would he kill yet another man?

"Donovan! Tom Donovan!" The insistent call echoed through the night over the sounds of the creaking wagon and racing hoof beats.

Dad reared back, slowing the wagon to a stop, his profile grim in the moonlight as he peered around the canvas covering. He gripped the pistol and brought it in front of him.

Katie reached for her little sister and held her close. Susannah looked up at her with wide, innocent eyes. Katie put her finger over her lips to silence the little girl and trembled for what might happen.

The two men pulled to a stop at the front of the wagon. As the closest man turned toward her father, the moon caught and held in its light the glint of a Silver Star pinned to his vest.

"Howdy, Sheriff. Deputy." Dad nodded to them. "You're a bit far from town tonight, aren't you?"

"I thought that was you, Donovan." The sheriff's deep voice sent a shiver down Katie's spine. "We stopped by your place first. Musta just missed you."

Dad's shoulders moved.

Please, Lord, don't let him shoot them.

"Thought we had an agreement, Donovan, that you was to stay close to home." The sheriff peered around the corner of the canvas cover and nodded at Mama. "Howdy, ma'am."

Mama's smooth white skin seemed even paler than usual with her bright blue eyes wide and pleading. "My husband didn't mean to kill anyone, Sheriff. He was protecting our home."

"Your husband had no home to protect when he bashed Mr. Hiram Bentley's head against the iron post in front of the saloon, ma'am. Several witnesses said he lost your property fair and square in the poker game."

Mama's head bowed. "I understand, but if you'll let us go on to Oregon, we'll be out of your jurisdiction, so you won't have to worry about Tom again. I'm sure he's learned his lessons—about drinking and gambling."

The sheriff looked back at Dad. "Is that right, Donovan? Are you giving up spirits and cards?"

The deputy's snicker irritated Katie. He had no right to laugh, true though it was Dad had a weakness toward drink. How many times had they moved because he couldn't hold down a job more than a few months before getting into some kind of scrape?

Dad's good-natured grin lit his face. "Sure, Sheriff, that's what I promised my wife I'd do. A new home in a new land is what I need."

"Maybe you're right, Donovan." The sheriff looked past Tom. "Ma'am, I'm sorry you lost your home. Mr. Hiram Bentley did not die. He got a little bump on his head is all. I'm leaving this rascal in your custody. I wish you the best in getting him straightened out."

"Thank you, Sheriff." Mama's face relaxed.

The sheriff nodded. "You got away with it this time, Donovan, but next time it might not be so easy. The next man you hit in a drunken fit may not make it and then where will your family be? What about those two boys of yours? What kind of example—"

The sheriff leaned closer and peered into the wagon. He turned and looked down the road. "By the way, where are they?"

Dad shifted. "They went ahead with the cattle."

"So, you really are headin' for Oregon?"

"Yep. Not much left for us now."

"No, I guess not." The sheriff touched the brim of his hat and nodded toward Mama. "We'll be gettin' back to town. Hope you find what you're looking for out West."

~*~

How far was it from Jefferson City to Independence? Seemed they'd been traveling forever and they were only now reaching the start of their journey—the beginning of the Oregon Trail. Katie sloshed through another mud puddle and glared at the same gray cover they'd traveled under for days. Spring showers had been their constant companion across western Missouri, and the longer she trudged through mud and water, the more she longed for a warm, soaking bath.

After traveling alone for so long, the busyness and noise of Independence came as a shock. Katie's eyes opened wide at all the men, women, and children. The drizzling rain seemed to have no effect on any of them. Shaggy-haired mountain men shuffled past wearing buckskins. Riverboat captains, dockworkers, soldiers, and traders filled the streets, shouting to each other as they went about their business.

There were so many Indians. Dressed like white men or wrapped in old-looking blankets, they lounged in front of stores. What were they doing in town? One rode a shaggy brown and white pony past her so close she could have touched him. Instead, she shrank back. The Indian didn't even look, and still her heart pounded out of control. She walked beside the wagon, looking from side to side half expecting one of the savages to jump out at her with bow and arrow ready or a tomahawk raised.

Katie breathed a sigh of relief when the wagon stopped in front of a large house not far from Main Street. A sign in the front yard said, "Miller's Boardinghouse."

Dad's voice sounded tired. "Let's see if we can get rooms here. We need a place to stay a few days before we join a wagon train. In the meantime we'll stock up and get ready to go."

Katie looked at the two-story, white framed house that would be their temporary home. A boardinghouse wasn't as luxurious as a hotel, but it should have the necessities they'd been forced to do without since they'd been on the run. At the moment, only two things mattered. A bath and a clean bed.

~*~

Katie glanced out the upstairs window as two men in a wagon turned off the road. The man driving stopped behind the boardinghouse, and her older brother, Tommy, helped their mother climb down from the back of the men's wagon.

Katie leaned out the window as the four walked across the yard to the Donovan's covered wagon. The men climbed in the back and soon began unloading—no! She covered her mouth with her hand to stifle a cry of alarm as the men pulled Mama's rosewood organ from the wagon. She ran from the room and down the stairs. Mama's organ was an heirloom. Grandmother Duvall had owned that organ and given it to Mama on her wedding day. No one could play an organ as well as her mama. What could she be thinking? With the farm gone, it was the only remaining tie to her childhood.

Katie burst through the back door as the wagon holding the organ rolled out of the yard and into the road behind the boardinghouse. "Mama, your organ. Stop them. They can't take it."

She ran past Mama and Tommy to the road, her heart pounding unmercifully. She couldn't catch them. She ran back to her mother. "Mama, why did you give them your organ? How could you?"

Tears blurred her vision, but not so much she couldn't see the matching tears in her mother's eyes. Mama held her arms

4

out and Katie stepped into her embrace. "I know, honey. I know. I feel the same way, but I had to."

"Why, Mama?"

Mama pulled back and captured Katie's gaze with her own. She reached out and pulled Tommy into the embrace. "Because the money will be needed more. This move to Oregon will be hard." She looked from one to the other. "Tommy, you will be nearing twenty-one by the time you set foot in Oregon. Katie, you are nineteen already—old enough to marry and start a family of your own. As hard as our journey will be for all of us, I fear it will be hardest on the two of you."

Katie brushed off Mama's dire words. Their beautiful organ—gone. This was Dad's fault. She wiped the tears that wouldn't stop falling. First their farm and now Mama's organ had been taken from them. What more damage could he do to the family? She huffed. What indeed? There was nothing more of value remaining for them to lose.

Mama's nanny goat, staked a few feet away, lifted her head and bleated. Katie glared at her. If Mama wanted money, why hadn't she sold the goat instead of her organ?

~*~

"Here, Bossy." Jason Barnett touched the side of his employer's milk cow with a stick to guide her toward the holding ground near camp. The heifer trotted along beside. Mr. Taylor hadn't been feeling well this morning or he'd have taken the cows himself.

The Taylors were like parents to him. When they took the notion to move to Oregon, there was no stopping them. Not that he'd tried all that hard. He liked the idea, but he was young and healthy. They were—well, old enough to be his parents. He wanted his own land, but he wouldn't dessert Mr. and Mrs. Taylor to get it. They'd have to come to some agreement once they reached Oregon.

"There you go, Bossy." Jason patted the Guernsey on the rump and let her join the other cattle in the holding pen. Once they got on the trail, things were bound to be different. Poor Bossy might have to be tied to the back of the wagon while they traveled. He'd wait and see how things were handled after the meeting later today.

"Yahoo." A boy on a spirited horse raced past. He circled back and joined a small herd of cattle being driven by a man.

Jason watched them drive their cattle into the pen. One contrary cow lumbered his direction, obviously trying to avoid confinement. Jason ran toward her and waved his stick. His actions seemed to change her mind as she pivoted and went into the pen.

"Hey, thanks, Mister. Calamity gets ornery." The boy called out. He jerked the reins and the horse made a quick turn.

Jason froze in place as boy and horse went down in the mud beside the creek that ran next to the pen. Before they hit the ground, he started running toward them, his heart pounding. The journey hadn't even started. He prayed aloud as he ran. "Lord, please don't let him be hurt. Keep the horse from falling on him."

~*~

"Westport is just ahead." Katie's father called out over the noise of the wagon rattling down the muddy dirt road. "This is where we should be able to hook up with a train going to Oregon."

"Come, Suzy." Katie took her little sister's hand and pulled her toward the front opening of the wagon where they could see. Thankfully, the drizzling rain of that morning had stopped. As the wagon crested the top of a slight rise in the road, Katie caught her breath. White from many canvas-topped wagons, spread haphazardly across several acres of land, shone in the morning sun. A mass of people moved about attending to one task or another. It was as if they'd stumbled upon a village on wheels. What would these people be like? In the next six months of travel, they'd be in close contact and would without doubt make many friends or enemies.

So many families moving out West was hard to understand. Why would they go? Surely each had their own story. "Manifest Destiny." She breathed the words under her breath.

What did it mean? That the United States was destined to expand clear to the Pacific Ocean, and her family would be part of it. To imagine the United States becoming so large was almost unbelievable, yet just looking at all the people gathered here filled Katie's mind with the possibility. If so many were willing to pull up roots and take off across a wilderness that promised danger to reach an unknown land, then others would follow. Yet not everyone was going because they wanted to. How many had been forced to go, as her family had?

Contagious excitement vibrated in the air, dimming Katie's resentment. There was too much to see and experience to harbor anger. Her heart swelled with the thought that she was a pioneer in much the same way as her ancestors had been almost a century before.

"This looks like a good spot." Dad guided the oxen to the left and stopped under a maple tree.

A breeze shook several drops of water from the leaves above their heads as they climbed from the wagon. Katie grabbed Susanna's hand and laughing with her, ran a few steps away to keep from getting wet. She lifted Susanna and twirled with her.

"Whoa there."

A deep voice startled her. She stopped just short of bumping into a man. Another twirl and Susanna's feet would have hit him. He caught her by the shoulders to steady her. She let her sister slide to the ground.

"Katie, you almost knocked Jason down." Katie's younger brother, Karl, ran toward them with a disapproving look on his freckled face.

"Oh, I'm sorry." Katie stepped back as Jason released her. "Suzy and I were just getting away from the rain dripping out of the tree."

Susanna's laughter caught her attention. "You look like a drownded rat."

Katie looked at her brother and noticed that his clothes and hair were soaked.

"What happened to you?" She turned to her mother. "Mama, look at Karl. I knew he was too young to let run free."

Mama stepped closer. "What happened, Karl?"

Karl's eyes shone with excitement. "I was on Star, and she slipped when we put the cows in the holding pen. I fell in the mud, but Jason came and helped me. He held my horse while I took a bath in the creek. I knew you wouldn't want me to come back all muddy."

"Of course not." Mama put her fingers over her mouth.

"You took a bath in your clothes?" Susanna's blue eyes grew wide. "We aren't supposed to do that, are we, Mama?"

Karl's grin grew even bigger. "Yeah, I took a bath and washed my clothes all at the same time. Good idea, huh?"

Susanna giggled. Katie crossed her arms and shook her head. What her little brother wouldn't think of doing would scarcely be worth mentioning. She often wondered how her mother could put up with his shenanigans.

Tommy, Katie's older brother, strode into camp and spoke to his father. "We got the animals taken care of. There's a holding pen just outside camp where everyone's putting their cattle and extra horses. We'll be taking turns keeping watch over them. Once we're on the trail, though, each family will be required to drive their own animals."

"Sounds fair to me. Have you talked to anyone to know who's in charge? If they let you put your animals in the pen they must have room for us."

Tommy nodded. "It's a large company. I think they figure there's safety in numbers. There's a man, Jeb Larson, who's the guide. I was told there's to be a meeting this afternoon to elect a wagon master."

Dad nodded. "All right. We'll be there. Let's get this wagon unhitched."

Katie's attention moved back to her mother as she spoke to Karl's new friend. "I appreciate you helping my son and I'm pleased to meet you, Mr. . . .?"

"Barnett, Ma'am, but please call me Jason. I didn't do anything. Just helped Karl to his feet and held his horse while he got the mud off."

"You've made quite an impression on him."

Jason shrugged. "From what I've seen, Karl's a pretty special boy." He reached out and ruffled Karl's red hair. "Glad I could help."

Karl ducked, but not before Katie saw the pleased

expression on his face. Mr. Barnett had made a friend for life, whether he wanted it or not.

Mama turned toward her soaked son. "You get in the wagon and change into something dry. Go now before you catch a cold."

Katie stepped back as her mother and brother left. She glanced at the young man who looked as if he'd rather be anywhere else at the moment. His blond hair contrasted with bronzed skin apparently no stranger to the sun. The effect was striking. Muscles, obviously toned and strengthened by hard labor, rippled beneath his blue cotton shirt. He was not the most handsome man she'd ever seen, but something about him drew her. Of course, his coloring would attract anyone's attention.

Jason turned. His eyes met Katie's and held. She lowered her gaze, but not before she saw the intensity in his gray eyes as if he were trying to read her thoughts.

A flush warmed her face, and she turned away. They would soon need a fire. She began gathering sticks.

"May I be of assistance, Miss Donovan?" Jason's voice was much too close.

She dropped her sticks into a pile and shook her head. "I'm sure I can build a fire."

He tossed more sticks with hers then stepped back.

Katie arranged the smallest twigs on the ground. She took a match from their newly purchased supply and struck it against a rock. Cupping her hands carefully around the flame, she held it against the kindling. Her feeble flame went out.

If Karl's friend would leave, she might be able to get the fire started. Her hands trembled as she reached for a second match.

Jason squatted beside her and picked up a small stick. Katie turned enough to see his hands. He opened a pocketknife and cut a pile of shavings from the stick. Without permission, he plucked the second match from her fingers and struck it on the rock she'd used earlier. Using the shavings as kindling, his fire sprang to life.

Warmth rose to Katie's cheeks. Who did this man think he was, coming into their camp and taking over as if he belonged there? She sprang to her feet, planted her hands on her hips, and opened her mouth to tell him her opinion of brash young men.

"Oh, how nice, Mr. Barnett." Mama hurried toward them. "You got our fire started. To tell you the truth, I wondered if we could. Everything's so wet. God must have sent you our way. First Karl and now this."

She bestowed a warm, motherly smile on Jason. Katie clenched her teeth. Make that two conquests for Mr. Barnett. First Karl and now Mama.

"We'll soon have our noon meal. Won't you stay and take it with us?"

Jason turned with a broad smile. "Thank you, ma'am, but I'll have to come another time. I'm expected at my own camp for nooning. I'm sure I'll hear about it if I'm late, too." He laughed and with a wave that included them all, he turned and left.

Katie's air whooshed from her lungs. He was expected at his own camp? So he was a married man? An irrational sense of loss took the place of her anger. There had been something different about Mr. Barnett. Something powerful and sure. She couldn't put her finger on it, but Jason Barnett was different from any other young man she'd met, and that intrigued her.

"Tommy, before you go, could you set up a spit on either side of this fire so I can hang a pot from it?" Mary called to her oldest son as he started off with his father.

"Sure." Tommy grabbed a hammer and the iron bars that made the spit then anchored it in the ground.

He spoke in an undertone to Katie. "I heard there's going to be a dance tonight. Wagon trains almost always do that the night before they head out."

Katie's eyes widened. "You'll take me, won't you?"

Tommy shrugged and grinned. "Figured I would."

Chapter 2

*K*atie wiped the last plate to the sound of a guitar thrumming and someone tuning a banjo. She hurried to stow the clean dishes away. The disjointed notes soon merged into a lively tune of invitation to the many campfires twinkling in the gathering dusk of evening. Her toes tapped with the urge to dance. She ran to the edge of their camp as others nearby headed toward the music.

She twirled toward her older brother leaning against a maple tree. "Tommy, are you ready to go? This may be our last chance to have fun for a long time."

Tommy hopped up and bowed low. "At your service, Ma'am."

"You aren't going to a dance our first night out, are you?" Mama sat in her rocker with mending in her lap.

Dad perched on an upright barrel, whittling. He shook his head. "Oh, let them have a little fun. Katie's right. There'll not be time for socializing once we get under way. Tonight is the time to get acquainted with our traveling mates."

Mama's eyebrows drew together as she picked up her sewing again.

Katie took Tommy's arm and almost skipped across the grass to where several couples were already dancing. A crowd of spectators stood in a circle around the dancers and watched.

"Are you going to dance with me?" Tommy glanced to the side where some young men stood. "Or do you want one of them?"

Katie tossed her head. "I'll start with you. If anyone else wants to dance with me, he'll ask."

Tommy chuckled. "My poor, shy sister. I'll bet you don't even know what a wallflower is."

"Of course, I do." Katie smiled and kept her steps in time with her brother's. She loved to dance and seldom sat out. She knew what a wallflower was, she'd just never been one.

As the first dance ended, a tall, handsome man with dark hair stepped forward. "May I have the next dance?"

The dimple that flashed in his cheek caught Katie's attention. She moved from her brother without a second thought.

"I'm Clay Monroe. And you are?" He took her hand.

"Katie Donovan." She turned, but Tommy had already walked away. "That was my brother, Tommy Donovan."

"I thought I saw a family resemblance." He grinned. "Facial features, not hair color. Did you know your hair looks like burgundy wine sparkling in the sunshine?"

"Wine?" Katie laughed. "Is that a compliment?"

"Most certainly." He drew back as if offended. "I'm partial to wine."

Katie lifted her eyebrows. "You're a drunkard?"

He threw back his head and laughed. "That's a good one. No, Katie Donovan, I'm not. I seldom drink. A glass rarely, which may be why I enjoy it."

Katie relaxed and enjoyed Clay's company. His steps were sure and smooth, his conversation as lively as the music that surrounded them. Her feet kept time, and she couldn't remember when she'd had more fun. When the dance ended, she moved to another partner, but kept Clay in sight.

He headed her way as soon as that second dance ended. "Hey, my turn again." He stepped between Katie and the other fellow.

She didn't mind.

He took her hand in his and bent close to her. "I've decided to dance with you the rest of the evening. What do you think about that?"

She pulled back to look into his eyes. "I don't know. It doesn't sound like you're asking."

He grinned. "I'm not."

The music started before she could think of a good response, and Clay swept her toward him as they danced in

12

perfect rhythm. He pulled her closer than she was used to, but when she tried to step back, his arm tightened. He leaned near and spoke in a low voice. "Did you know you are very beautiful, Katie Donovan?"

A flush rose in Katie's cheeks. "Are you trying to turn my head, Clay Monroe?"

"Oh, no." His dimple flashed. "I'm stating a fact."

Excitement bubbled within Katie. If only he would loosen his hold on her. She pushed back as if making light of his compliment. "Oh, really? You're trying to flatter me because we dance so well together."

He laughed. "That may be."

His face grew serious as he looked into her eyes. He again tightened his arm around her, his hand splayed across the back of her waist. "You really are beautiful." His voice rumbled low and soft next to her ear.

Katie caught her breath. Never had a man looked at her in such a way. Or held her so close. Mama would say this is what came of dancing. She laughed and tossed a strand of long hair from her face while she eased back. "You're trying to turn my head and it won't work."

"Oh, really? Then how can I turn your head?"

"You can't."

"Oh, but I will some way. I intend to win you over before we're half way to Oregon. You do know that, don't you?" Clay grinned. "I'll watch, Katie, and find out what you like, then I'll win your heart."

"Win me? For what purpose?" Katie kept her voice light despite the pounding of her heart. Could he hear it?

Clay's hand caressed Katie's. "What do you think? I'm twenty-one and on my way to Oregon to claim land. I'm ready to marry, Katie, and I think you're the girl I want."

Clay rested his cheek against Katie's as he held her tight in his arms. His words ran through her mind, but before she could sort them out, he lifted his head and stopped dancing. She looked up to see her brother had cut in.

An angry frown drew Tommy's brows together. He took her arm and pulled her away from Clay, then stepped between the two of them before she realized what was happening. Clay's face looked as shocked as she felt.

"What's the matter with you, Tommy?"

"Hey, what're you doing?"

"I'm her brother." Tommy answered Clay as if being her brother gave him the right. He turned his back on Clay and whirled her away.

Clay stood with a stunned expression on his face. Katie's mind whirled. She still hadn't absorbed Clay's outlandish proposal. Or proclamation. Or whatever it was. And now this. She caught her breath and matched her steps to her brother's. Should she be angry or grateful? "Why'd you do that?"

Tommy scowled. "That fellow was practically pawing you, and you acted like you were enjoying it. That's why."

She tossed her head. "I can take care of myself."

Tommy snorted. "Sure, you can take care of yourself. Right into trouble."

Katie stopped short, jerked away, and lifted her chin. "Thank you so much, Tommy, for rescuing me. Now that you've ruined my evening, I'll go back to the wagon and turn in early. That's what you wanted anyway, isn't it?"

"Oh, Katie, why do you have to be so hot-headed?" Tommy shook his head. "You don't even know when I do you a favor."

"Some favor." She swung away from her brother. Clay no longer stood where they'd left him. She searched through the gathering and didn't see him. He'd probably forget that ridiculous proposal, if that's what it was, soon enough. What she had said was the truth. Her evening was ruined now. She headed toward the wagon. And hesitated.

Standing at the edge of a group of onlookers was Karl's new friend, Jason Barnett. His gaze caught hers and held. There was that awful feeling of having her inner thoughts revealed. How did he do that? He had no idea how she felt or what she believed in.

He didn't smile or turn away. He looked at her with a sad expression as if he pitied her. Or maybe his eyes held disappointment as Mama's often did. Maybe he'd seen her dancing with Clay. He had no right to accuse her of wrong doing. Mama and Karl might think he was wonderful, but she didn't.

She walked on, yet her gaze shifted to either side of him. He stood in a group of men. Ha! He'd left his wife back at camp while he watched the dance. If so, he had no business condemning her. She turned away with the intention of ignoring him if their paths crossed again. In fact, she wouldn't even waste her time thinking about him. Yet when she climbed into the wagon and lay on the narrow straw mat topping a row of boxes that served as her bed, scenes of Jason Barnett and Clay Monroe intermingled in her mind until she finally fell into a restless sleep.

~*~

"Well, this is it." Dad called over his shoulder. He picked up the reins and settled on the wagon seat.

Katie took a quick breath and let it out in a rush as their wagon jerked forward. She peeked out the back end of the wagon into early morning confusion as so many wagons prepared to begin the long trail to Oregon. Susanna cuddled close to her, her blue eyes darting back and forth as she looked from one wagon to another in the long line behind them.

Confusion certainly was a good word to describe what was going on. With all the abrupt starts and stops of the wagons it was obvious that most of the drivers didn't know what they were doing. The newly elected wagon master, Jack Colton, along with Jeb Larson, rode their horses up and down, shouting instructions and encouragement to the men who were trying to position the wagons into four columns, seventeen wagons long. Sixty-eight wagons in all. Katie still had trouble realizing so many people wanted to move west. Finally, the wagons gained a resemblance of order and the train began its slow trek out of Missouri.

"Do we have to sit here all day?" Susanna's lower lip stuck out.

Katie stretched. She was tired of riding too. "No, we can walk if you want to."

Susanna sat up straight and peeked over the tailgate. She

turned big, blue eyes on Katie. "The wagon's moving."

"We'll be careful." Jumping out of a moving wagon, especially with another rolling toward them was a dangerous thing to do, but Katie didn't care. Dad couldn't stop for them so she gathered her skirt close and climbed over the backboard. When her toes touched the edge of the frame, she lowered herself until she could jump nimbly to the ground. When she caught her balance, she walked behind, keeping pace, with her arms out toward her little sister.

"Come on, Suzy. Reach for me, and I'll lift you out."

Susanna didn't hesitate and soon stood on the ground with Katie. "That was fun, wasn't it?"

Katie pulled her to the side away from the wagons. "Yes, but don't you ever do that without me or Tommy to help you. Do you promise, Suzy?"

Susanna looked up at her with wide, solemn eyes and nodded. "I promise."

Mama's nanny goat tied to the backside of the wagon bleated at them as if adding her warning to Katie's. Or more likely threatening them if they didn't move on.

Katie looked up at the overcast sky and took Susanna's hand. "Come on, Suzy. Let's walk in the grass away from the wagons."

By the time the call for nooning sounded, Katie longed to sit and relax. Instead she helped Mama get out the leftovers from breakfast and the night before. Every muscle ached to relax, but it was not to be. After they ate, the dishes had to be cleaned and put away.

In spite of her lack of rest, Katie searched the company for either Jason or Clay throughout the afternoon and saw neither man. Both intrigued her. Clay because of his bold proposal. Jason because he seemed so mysterious. If he had a wife, he kept her hidden.

That evening, Katie sat in camp with the rest of her family. She fixed a plate for Susanna and another for Karl while Mama fixed for Dad and Tommy.

"We had it easy today, I hear." Dad took his plate from Mama and sat on the barrel he'd rolled from the wagon for a chair. "Colton and Larson made our first day on the trail as easy as possible."

"Easy?" Katie couldn't stop the word from leaving her lips. She longed for a decent bed where she could rest. Even a chair to relax in would be wonderful, but Mama's rocker was all they'd brought.

Dad laughed. "You aren't the only one who thinks that way. From here on, we can expect to put in a full day's travel." He rubbed his hands together and looked at Mama. "Let's eat and get bedded down quick as we can. Tomorrow will come soon enough."

Katie had no argument with him this time.

After she helped Mama clear the meal away and wash the dishes, Mama read a few verses from her Bible. As soon as she closed the cover and put her Bible away, Katie took Susanna to the wagon. Never had bed looked so inviting. Even Susanna didn't dawdle.

~*~

The blast of a bugle jerked Katie from a sound sleep. She sat up and stretched before opening her eyes to the dark interior of the wagon.

"It's still the middle of the night. It's pitch black in here," she grumbled.

Her mother's soft voice came through the darkness. "It will become light soon enough. There's so much to do before we can start the wagons moving."

Katie watched the dark silhouette of her mother as she climbed out the back of the wagon. With a sigh, she reached for the dress she had placed beside her the night before. The lumpy straw mattress barely held both her and Susanna. She jumped down from the crates that made up her bed to the narrow aisle in the middle of the floor. She pulled her dress on, letting the cotton material fall around her. Getting dressed in the dark was not something she looked forward to doing for the next six months, but she refused to sleep in her dress. It would wrinkle terribly, and even if no one else cared what she looked like, she certainly did.

The smell of brewing coffee and frying bacon penetrated

the wagon. The silence of the night faded with one voice after another calling out some word of instruction or greeting. The entire camp came alive in the space of a few minutes.

A loud smack on the end of the wagon made Katie jump. "Hey, you girls, get a move on." Dad called to her. "This is your last morning to sleep in. The boys are already up and working."

Katie clenched her jaw tight to keep from saying something she would regret. She rolled her eyes and made a face toward the end opening, knowing her father would never know of her rebellious feelings. Maybe there was an advantage to this darkness after all.

"I'm about ready," she called out to him.

His footsteps sounded as he moved away.

She stood by her bed to help Susanna dress. "Turn, sweetie, so I can fasten these tiny buttons down your back."

"Katie, what's wrong? Why am I having to get up at night?" Susanna's voice sounded small and sleepy in the darkness.

"Because we'll be traveling today, and we need breakfast first."

"I'm not hungry." Susanna lay back down. "I'm sleepy."

Katie looked down at the dark spot of her sister against the white sheet. What help would a sleepy five-year-old child be, anyway? She didn't care what her father said. Susanna needed to sleep more than she needed to be outside in the way. She turned toward the rear of the wagon.

The cool night air hit her as soon as she stepped down. She rubbed her arms and joined her mother who stood adding wood to the glowing coals she had raked out of the bed of ashes. A fire soon blazed, and Mama started the side meat frying. Katie stifled a yawn as she reached for the dishes to help her mother get breakfast ready and dished out for the family. She worked quickly. She needed to get Suzy up before her father and brothers returned.

Soon breakfast was ready, and Susanna sat on the ground picking at her biscuit, bacon, and mush. Katie knew exactly how she felt.

Dad stuffed his last bite of biscuit in his mouth and stood. "Katie, your mama needs some help. You best be getting the dishes clean for her."

Katie bristled at his command. "I do help Mama. Who do you think washed the dishes last night?"

"Of course you help." Mama defended her.

Dad shook his head. "I know you help, but Mama needs more help now than ever. She's not able to do it all herself. You see that you pitch in every chance you get, and Susanna can help you."

Katie didn't answer. Dad had changed. This move was his fault, yet he never said he was sorry that she'd heard.

He left with Tommy and Karl to get the oxen.

She watched Mama kick a stick of wood away from the fire. Had Dad changed so much from the kind, gentle father she knew, or was something more wrong? Something her father knew but didn't want to say.

Mama hadn't been sick other than an occasional headache for a long time. Not since before Susanna was born. Surely it couldn't be another baby. She and Tommy were grown. Mama should be too old to have babies. The blood drained from her head with the thought. What else could it be? Dad had to have known before they left home. Even when he was at the saloon gambling away their farm.

Anger surged, bringing blood to pound in her temples. How Mama put up with him, she'd never understand. No man should be so irresponsible to gamble away their farm with his wife in the family way. Didn't he understand the risk of a woman giving birth on a journey such as this? In her condition, she could die even before the birthing and likely would. Six months on the trail, and if Mama and Dad already knew, that meant the baby would be born before they reached Oregon.

She stood and grabbed the water bucket. Fueled by an anger that continued to boil in her heart, she stomped off toward the creek scarcely aware of Susanna running along behind.

Chapter 3

*L*ight from a campfire someone had built near the bank of the water guided Katie's steps. She met several already heading back to camp, but others were still there. So many feet had stirred up the bank until it was soft with mud, which didn't improve Katie's mood.

"Can I wash dishes, too?"

Katie barely glanced at her sister. "I don't care. Let me get some water first. We'll have to take it back and heat it."

After scooping water from the creek into her bucket, she started back the way they'd come. Although no glow yet lit the sky, the sun would soon be up. She stepped out with long strides, trying to hold the bucket level so it wouldn't splash out on her skirt. Susanna ran along beside her, but she couldn't slow down. If she didn't get the dishes done, Dad would think she'd been dawdling.

"Good morning." A woman near her own age spoke as they met on the path.

Katie glanced at the other girl and nodded. "Hello."

She and Susanna hurried on. By the time they warmed the water and had the dishes done, a rosy glow touched the eastern horizon, chasing the darkness of night away. Katie hurried to put everything in its place so her mother would have as little to do as possible.

She bent to stow the last dish in the storage space under the bed of the wagon when a hard bump from behind sent her sprawling on the ground.

"Katie, are you hurt?" Her mother's exclamation and Susanna's giggles came from the wagon.

The bleat of her mother's goat told her what had happened.

"Nanny doesn't like it when you bend over, Katie."

20

Susanna giggled even more.

"I'm fine. Why is that goat loose, anyway? I'm dirty now." Katie started to push herself off the ground when she heard a male voice that belonged to neither Tommy nor her father.

"Whoa there."

She hesitated, still on her hands and knees, as she recognized not only the voice, but also the expression. Her heart sank. Jason Barnett. What did he do? Go around looking for people to help? Or torment.

"Miss, I think it might be a good idea to go ahead and get up. I'm having a hard time holding your goat back." He coughed. "She's wanting to . . ."

Katie's face burned as she finished pulling herself to her feet. She'd never felt so awkward. When she glanced at Jason, he had his back to her as he talked to her mother. She puffed out the breath she'd been holding.

"This is a nanny goat, isn't it? I didn't know nannies were inclined to butt."

Mama smiled. "I don't think they usually do. Our Nanny is an unusual goat, but she gives a lot of milk. Enough to share if you would like some?"

Jason shrugged. "Sure, if you have extra. I think Mr. Taylor likes it."

Katie frowned at his back. There he went again, doing good. He couldn't take the milk for himself. Might as well make two good deeds out of one. He wouldn't want to stop with rescuing her. No, he had to get milk for someone else. While she fumed, he tied Nanny to the side of the wagon and left with a jar of milk.

Why'd Mama have to bring her nanny goat with them, anyway? The rest of the family would have preferred leaving her behind. Katie brushed at the dirt on her skirt and glowered at the goat. Maybe Nanny would come up missing somewhere along the trail. But no, Mama would be heartbroken. For some reason she seemed quite fond of her contrary goat.

~*~

With the sun still low in the sky, the bugle sent forth clear notes signaling another day of travel. Katie helped Susanna climb in the back of the wagon and took her place beside her sister where they could watch out the opening.

The Donovan wagon occupied space in an outer column near the end of the line, which meant it would be several days before their turn came to ride in the lead. In the meantime, they would be traveling through the billowing clouds of dust kicked up from those in front. Before long, Susanna would tire of sitting still and fighting the dust for a breath of clean air. When she did, Katie would walk with her.

Today, the wagons fell into line with less confusion than the day before. Dad's whip cracked in the air and he yelled at the oxen. "Get on there. Haw!"

Katie held to the edge of the tailgate as the wagon creaked and jolted into place. Before long, the wagon became warm and stuffy with dust settling over everything. Katie glanced toward the front of the wagon where Mama sat beside Dad. They might have more air, but it was probably even harder to breathe up there. Susanna lay back with her head on Katie's lap and played with her rag doll. She hadn't mentioned walking and Katie soon became cramped and bored. She tried stretching her legs out one at a time, but that helped very little.

Tommy and Karl were lucky. They got to ride herd on the cattle, using their two riding horses, Star and Midnight. It might be a hard, dirty job, but their freedom should more than make up for it. She looked out at the wagon following theirs.

A boy a few years younger than her sat on the driver's seat alone. He grinned and waved, his blond hair flying out in the breeze.

Katie waved at him as a girl climbed out through the front opening of his wagon and settled on the seat beside him. Katie squinted for a better look. She'd seen that girl someplace else. Yes. Just this morning on the way back from the creek. It was the girl who spoke to her. She'd seemed friendly, as if she'd like to be friends. Katie straightened and leaned out, extending her arm above her head to wave in large sweeping motions.

The girl smiled and returned Katie's wave. She called something, but the noise of the wagons and oxen whipped it away with the wind before Katie could hear. She cupped her hand around her ear and leaned forward. The girl pointed to the side of the trail and walked her two fingers along her arm.

Katie laughed. That she understood. She nodded and turned to Susanna. "Come on, Suzy. We're going to walk again."

"Okay." Susanna sat up and hugged her doll close. "Are we going to jump out the back again?"

"Yes, but we're going to be very careful doing it, because we don't want to get run over by those big oxen behind us. Are you ready?"

"Yes." Susanna looked at Katie with complete trust.

Katie shook her head. She didn't deserve such a sweet, little sister. She lifted her skirts just enough to climb over the tailgate. The vision of Mr. Barnett holding Nanny back from butting her almost made her lose her grip. She giggled. It'd be just her luck if he stood behind her now with her hanging half-in and half-out of the wagon.

She shoved the thought aside and concentrated on her feet. Certain they were free, she jumped backward to the ground. As she got her balance, she took a couple of running steps to keep up with the moving wagon and lifted her hands. "Okay, Suzy. Come on." Katie caught her sister under the arms and pulled her from the wagon then swung her around and set her down out of the way.

As soon as her feet touched the ground, Susanna gave a little skip, causing her long blond curls to bounce on her back. "Oh, this is lots better than that bumpy, old wagon, isn't it, Katie?"

Katie grabbed her hand and ran with her through the grass to the side. "Yes, it is. Look, Suzy, the grass is already tall enough to hide our shoes."

"Can I go pick some flowers with those girls, Katie?"

Splashes of color dotted the growing grasses in all directions as far as Katie could see. She looked where Susanna pointed. A couple of young girls walked together picking wild flowers as they moved along near two women. Their laughter and delightful chatter filled the air with happy sounds.

"Of course you may join them. Just be sure to stay where you can see me."

As Susanna ran off to play, Katie turned and found the other girl waiting.

Her face brightened with a sweet smile. "Hi, my name is Rachel Morgan. I'm glad you decided to walk with me."

Katie warmed to Rachel's friendly smile. "I'm Katie Donovan. I saw you at the creek this morning. I didn't expect you to be in the wagon right behind ours. I think someone else had that position yesterday."

Rachel laughed. "Probably my parents. My father decided to switch wagons today."

Katie stared at her. "You mean you have two wagons?"

Rachel nodded. "Yes. The second was for Uncle Joseph, but he died before we reached Missouri."

"I'm sorry." Katie saw pain in the other girl's eyes and felt uncomfortable.

Rachel's steps matched Katie's. "It's all right. He was ready to go. He wasn't really my uncle, but we lived on the same plantation."

"I thought I detected a Southern accent in your voice." Katie smiled. "Where are you from?"

"Mississippi. My father was the plantation overseer."

If not for the manners Mama had drilled into her, Katie would ask why a man would leave a good job to traipse across two thousand miles of—well, she didn't know what. She didn't want to think about it, either. "I thought I'd seen everyone our age at the dance the night before we started, but I don't remember seeing you there."

Rachel's smile caused tiny dimples to play beside each upward curve of her mouth in cheeks that were smooth and lightly tanned. Her olive complexion matched her dark brown hair and eyes, creating a lovely picture. Katie felt pale next to her.

"That's because I wasn't there."

"You weren't? Why not?"

Rachel shrugged. "I don't dance.

"You mean you don't know how? Or," Katie's eyes narrowed. Surely Rachel wasn't as old-fashioned as Mama. "Or, you don't believe in it?"

24

Rachel looked down before her eyes met Katie's. "Both. Dancing is probably not wrong, but other things. . ."

When her voice trailed off, Katie laughed. "You sound like my mother."

Rachel smiled, and Katie saw sincerity in her eyes. She shrugged. "Well, everyone to their own beliefs." She glanced to the side. "Is that your brother driving the wagon?"

Rachel nodded. "Yes, there's just the two of us—and our parents, of course."

"Four people and two wagons." Katie turned to see both wagons following Dad's and her stomach churned with longings she might as well forget.

Rachel laughed. "It still feels cramped sometimes."

Katie had never forged a bond with another girl as quickly as she did Rachel. Their differences were many, as were their beliefs, but that didn't seem to matter. She felt as if she'd known Rachel all her life by the time the sun crept high in the sky.

"Katie, I'm tired." Susanna ran across the grass and caught Katie's hand.

"I know. I am, too." Katie looked down at their feet. "Look, Suzy, our shadows are really short. That means we will stop for nooning right away."

Tommy rode Midnight past at a walk. He waved.

"See, Suzy, there's Tommy." She waved and so did Susanna. "Now I know it's almost time to eat. The wagons will be stopping soon."

"Tommy."

Katie looked up at Rachel's whisper and smiled.

Rachel didn't seem to notice, but turned to watch Tommy ride to the wagon and dismount. "Is he your brother?"

Katie nodded, although her friend didn't look her way. "Yes, he's the oldest. We have a younger brother named Karl. He's probably still with the cows."

Rachel didn't seem to hear, so Katie turned to Susanna. "The wagons are stopping now, Suzy. See if you can find Mama and tell her I'll be along shortly to help with the work."

As Susanna ran off, she called out to her, "Stay out of the

way of the wagons."

"Rachel?" Katie giggled when her new friend turned quickly. Two spots of pink appeared on her cheeks and she averted her eyes. So she found Tommy interesting, but she wouldn't embarrass her by mentioning the obvious. "I was just wondering if you'd like to walk with me again this afternoon?"

Rachel nodded and smiled. "Yes, that would be fine. I'll look forward to it." With that she turned and walked back toward her family's wagons.

Katie watched her go then headed toward Tommy and the wagon. What would he say if she told him he had an admirer?

Katie glanced over the company as drivers brought the wagons to a halt for the mid-day rest. With so many wagons blocking her sight and even more people milling about, she had no idea where Clay kept himself. For a young man determined to win her heart before they were halfway to Oregon, he needed to show his face once in a while. She'd seen Jason Barnett more than she'd seen Clay, and she felt certain Mr. Barnett had no such aspirations, although she doubted there was a Mrs. Barnett.

Chapter 4

*T*he next morning as Katie walked back from the creek with a bucket of water, someone fell into step with her.

"Hello, Katie, my love."

"Clay!" Her heart did a flip as she looked up at the handsome man. She hadn't seen him since the dance two days ago.

He grinned and stuck out his fist, which clutched several yellow flowers glistening with early morning dew. "I saw these and thought of you."

She took them and held them close for a sniff. A pleasant scent filled her senses. She smiled at him. "Thank you. Suzy has been picking flowers for the last two days, but she just throws them down when she gets tired of carrying them."

"Oh." He pouted like a little boy who came in last place. "I guess you've seen enough wild flowers to last you after walking in them for so long."

Katie laughed. "You don't know women very well, Clay Monroe. I never get tired of flowers. Besides, walking in them is nothing like being given a bouquet."

"From me, you mean?" An irresistibly impish grin pulled the corners of his mouth upward.

Again, she laughed. "Now why would they be any better coming from you than from my little sister?" She started walking slowly toward her parents' wagon.

He slipped the bucket from her hand and carried it. His voice lowered as he said, "If you don't know the answer to that—"

"So what's been keeping you busy the last two days?" Katie cut in before he said something she might not want to hear.

"Training to be a scout."

"A scout?" Katie stared at him. "What does that mean?"

"Jeb Larson asked me to ride with him. We go ahead of the train. He's showing me what to look and listen for, so I can warn him of any danger before the train rides into it."

"Oh." Katie searched his face and was satisfied he told the truth. "Is he expecting anything to happen?"

Clay shook his head. "Not here. That's why this is a perfect time to train. Your brother is going to start, too. He rode with us this morning."

"Tommy rode with you, and you didn't come to blows?" Katie laughed.

Clay grinned. "Nope. He really isn't such a bad guy as long as you aren't around."

"Well, thanks so much." She lifted her chin.

"Oh, don't worry about Tommy. He's just protective. I understand. I've got a little sister, too." He stopped short of the wagons. "I'd better git before Tommy sees me talking to you. Maybe in a day or two things will settle into a routine, and I can come see you when we camp for the night. Would you like that?"

She nodded, and he smiled. "Good, then I'll see you later."

She walked with Rachel that day, but the next morning, the overcast sky darkened, and a spring rain fell throughout the day. Katie and Susanna rode in the wagon where Katie read one of the two books she'd brought with her while Susanna played with her rag doll.

Although the rain slowed to an occasional sprinkle by the time they stopped to make camp, the fires were hard to start and kept going out because of the damp wood. Katie stared at the uncooperative fire. Jason Barnett built their fire with shavings from a small stick. She shrugged. It wouldn't hurt to try. She arranged the shavings and wood much like he'd done and struck a match. She laughed when it worked.

Jason had kept away since the day he rescued her from Nanny. In this big a company, his wagon could be anywhere. She set the water on to boil for beans and turned to search over the large circle of wagons as if she thought she might recognize his camp. Finally, she turned away, disgusted with her actions, and shoved Mr. Barnett from her mind. At least Clay was interested. He's the one she should think about.

"Katie, I don't know what I'd do without you." Mama pulled the iron skillet out of storage under the back of the wagon and carried it to the blazing fire. "I'm not much good at building fires."

Katie smiled at her mother. "In that case, I'll build the fires, and you can cook. You're much better at cooking than I am."

Mama poured cornbread batter in the skillet. "You wouldn't be flattering me so I'll agree to that, would you?"

"Of course not." Katie laughed. "Well, maybe a little, except it's the truth, too."

"Just a few more days and we should be at the Kansas River." Mama sighed. "I feel as if I've already been traveling a year."

Until then, Katie hadn't seen the signs of fatigue that shouldn't have been on Mama's face. The only thing she could do was take as much of the load on herself as possible. "Mama, why don't you go sit down? I can finish this."

Mama looked at Katie. "What happened to me doing all the cooking?"

"You know I was only joking. I can do this." Katie took the skillet from her mother, adjusted the lid on it, and set it over some hot coals she had scraped to the side earlier. Satisfied it sat level and the cornbread would bake, she stepped back.

Mama watched her. "We'll be crossing the river, you know."

Katie looked up at the strain in her mother's voice. It wasn't like her to worry about anything.

"Your dad said there will be a ferry to take us across and the animals will have to swim."

Katie smiled. "Good. I sure don't want to swim."

The hint of a smile touched Mama's lips. "No, I would think not."

~*~

Sometime during the night, another rain began and

continued without stopping until the day before they were to cross the Kansas River. Katie had never realized how miserable a gentle rain could make her life until then. So many chores had to be done outside, and the damp bedding needed to be aired.

Her spirits lifted the morning she stepped out of the wagon into sunshine streaming out from behind rapidly disappearing clouds. Maybe now they could dry out. As soon as they stopped for the night, she pulled the straw mattresses and the bedding out and laid them on a bush to air. Then, as had become her job, she started a fire for cooking.

Restlessness stirred within Katie. They'd been on the trail a week already in a company of well over two hundred people, and she'd met about as many people as she could count on one hand. The rain was mostly to blame for that. Not that knowing why made her feel any better. With all the work to be done, there was almost no time for socializing. After a full day of travel they were so exhausted by evening when they finally sat down to eat no one felt like visiting with a neighbor.

She selected some potatoes and a knife then glanced toward the camp next to theirs. It would be nice to encourage a friendship with Rachel, but if the week she'd just gone through was any indication of what the rest of the journey would be like, she'd spend the next six months with no one but Suzy for company.

"Hi."

Katie almost dropped her paring knife as she looked into Rachel's smiling face. She gripped the half-peeled potato in her other hand. "I didn't hear anyone coming. Sit down."

Rachel laughed.

Katie groaned. "I'm sorry. I guess we don't have a parlor here, do we?"

"Don't worry, Katie. I can't stay long anyway, and I've been sitting in the wagon for days what with all this rain. I just wanted to come over and speak to you. Maybe we can walk together again once we're across the Kansas River if the weather clears."

"I'm certainly ready for the rain to stop."

"Me, too." Rachel smiled. "I'll see you later. The rain

won't last forever. Let's take a walk tonight before dinner. Can you get away?"

"I'll make sure I do."

Katie's mood lifted from the brief contact with Rachel. That's all she needed. Friends who could help her forget the drudgery on this journey. Before long, they started across the rough ground laughing and talking. "Thanks for suggesting this walk, Rachel. I needed to get away without Suzy."

At Rachel's quick glance, she amended her comment. "I don't mean anything against my little sister. I love her dearly, but it's nice to be with someone my own age after being cooped up with a five-year-old for so long."

"I understand." Rachel smiled. "I've been around my little brother long enough the last few days. Do you want to take a look at the river?"

Katie shuddered, but shrugged off her fear of the water. "We might as well. We'll be crossing it tomorrow."

~*~

That evening as her family sat on the ground or leaned against the wagon eating rabbit stew, Katie felt more optimistic and content than she had thought possible.

Katie's younger brother, Karl, wolfed down his stew. He spoke around his last bite. "Tommy and me are going to swim the cows across the river tomorrow."

Mama's head jerked up, and her mending dropped into her lap while her brows drew together. "You'll do no such thing, Karl. It's too dangerous."

"Sure, we are, Mama." Karl puffed out his chest. "How do you think those cows will get across? We got to go with 'em so's they won't go off downstream."

"No," Mary shook her head. "You're too young."

"Mama!" The freckles on Karl's face stood out in the firelight. "I ain't too young. I'm twelve, almost thirteen."

"Karl, you aren't going in that river and that's final."

Katie had rarely heard her mother raise her voice to any of her children. She shrank from the sound and watched an angry flush cross Karl's face. He started to speak again, but their dad stopped him.

"That's enough, son. You'll obey your mother without another word." His voice softened then. "There'll be enough danger and excitement on the ferry."

Karl gave his father a long stare, his green eyes snapping. Then he swung on his heel and stomped away into the grayness of the evening. Mama started to call after him, but Dad stopped her. "Let him be, Mary. He'll be all right. He's got to learn to take no for an answer."

Katie watched the confrontation with her little brother in silence. Sounds of rushing water told her how close the river was. The spring rains that had made the past several days a trial for the wagon train had filled the river to overflowing.

When she and Rachel walked earlier, they'd gotten within sight of the water. The churning, rushing river frightened her. Why anyone would want to ride a horse into such a turbulent river was more than she could understand. But Karl was young and probably didn't understand the dangers involved. This entire journey was nothing more than an exciting adventure to him.

~*~

"Tomorrow won't be easy."

Jason looked up at Pa Taylor's comment. "No, I don't imagine it will. I've been wondering what I might do. I mean where I'd be of the most use."

"The wagons will ride the ferry, so I plan to handle ours." The older man looked out across the company, some still eating, others settling for the night. In the middle of the long ring of white-topped wagons, horses, oxen, and cattle milled about, grazing. He nodded toward them. "There's the big job, right there."

Jason followed his gaze. The animals would have to swim across. He'd seen the river and didn't like the thought. The spring rains they'd been putting up with weren't finished with them yet. Now instead of falling from the sky, soaking them and their bedding, the rushing water in the river would be an obstacle on their journey.

He nodded. "I'd offer my services, but I'd need a horse."

"Jason." The young voice demanded attention as Karl

Donovan ran into their camp. "Hey, Jason, what're you gonna do tomorrow?"

The boy's face was flushed as if he'd run a lap around the wagons. Jason chuckled. "Pa Taylor and I were just discussing that. I'm not sure what I can do, but I plan to help where there's need. It'll be a big day."

"Yeah." Karl plopped to the ground and crossed his arms over his bent knees. "Mama won't let me help take the cattle across."

Jason shared a smile with Pa Taylor. "Don't you think you're a little young to be doing a job like that?"

The boy's dark red eyebrows drew together. "That's what she said, and Dad agreed with her. Told me I have to ride in the wagon on the ferry with the girls."

"Give it time, Karl." Jason remembered the frustration of being too young. "You'll grow up soon enough. Enjoy the life God's given you now."

Karl's shoulders rose and fell with his sigh. "I guess."

He looked out at the moving mass of animals for a moment then straightened. "Hey, I know. Why don't you go in my place? You're old enough."

Jason grinned. "Yeah, I'm old enough, but I don't have a horse, Karl. A fellow swimming in that river wouldn't be much use. Probably wouldn't even make it across."

"No, I mean really take my place. I have a horse." Karl's face split into a huge grin. "You can ride Star."

A stirring of excitement brought Jason's head up as he looked into Karl's face. Maybe he could. If Mr. Donovan didn't mind. "Are you sure no one else will need your horse?"

"Who else is there? Katie's a girl and Tommy'll ride Midnight." Karl jumped to his feet. "Come on, let's go ask Dad. If you want to, I mean."

Jason turned to Pa Taylor. "What do you think?"

The older man rubbed his chin. "Won't be easy in that river. You're young and strong, and it's a needed job, but I'd sure hate it if you got hurt. Still, I see the eager light in your eyes. I guess it's your call."

"Thanks, Pa." Jason clapped a hand on Pa Taylor's

shoulder. "I'll see what Mr. Donovan says and go from there. I promise to be careful."

Jason draped an arm around Karl's shoulders as they left.

~*~

Katie looked up when Karl swaggered back into camp with a big grin on his face. She shifted her gaze to his side where Mr. Barnett stood. She set her empty bowl aside as her stomach took an unexpected flip.

"Mama, can Jason have some supper? He wants to talk to Dad."

Katie covered her mouth to keep from laughing at Mr. Barnett's obvious discomfort at Karl's question. A flush crept up his neck where his shirt lay open.

"Mrs. Donovan, please, I had no intention of barging in on you folks right when you're eating. I've already—"

"Nonsense." Mama ladled stew into two bowls and handed one to him and the other to Karl. "You're completely welcome. Go on over with the men folk and eat until you're full. There's plenty. Tommy got us some rabbits for stew."

Karl didn't wait for Jason, but sat on the ground in front of Dad and Tommy to eat his second bowl of stew that night. He didn't act as if he'd only minutes before left in a huff. He leaned toward Dad. "Jason wants to ride Star in the river tomorrow instead of me."

Tommy laughed and tousled Karl's red hair. "Reckon he thinks you're not big enough to carry him across?"

Karl jerked away. "That ain't what I meant, and you know it."

"Mr. Donovan, maybe I'd better explain." Jason settled on the ground beside Karl. "I work for Mr. and Mrs. Taylor and usually drive their wagon. I've talked to Mr. Taylor. With the river out of its banks the way it is, there will be a need for men on horseback guiding the livestock across. He wants to drive his own wagon so that leaves me free. Except, I don't have a horse."

Dad nodded. "Sounds like a good plan to me. Star doesn't have a rider. It might as well be you as another."

"Thank you, sir. I really appreciate this."

34

Dad looked at Jason. "You may not be thanking me after tomorrow. That won't be any picnic out there."

He jerked his head toward his oldest son. "Tommy will be riding Midnight. Both of you just remember to keep your heads about you. After all this rain there's bound to be whirlpools and rapids that'll suck you under before you know what's hit you."

"Yes, sir. I'll remember."

Jason visited a short while before leaving. As he rose to go, he turned to Mama. "Mrs. Donovan, thank you for a delicious meal."

She smiled. "You're welcome. I hope you'll join us again soon."

"Can I go show Star to Jason?" Karl pushed in beside him.

"Might be a good idea." Dad nodded. "Get acquainted with her before you get in the water."

Katie followed Jason's every move as he told her parents good-bye and left with Karl, but he never spared her a glance. She'd been so sure he was married, but now she didn't think so. He said he worked for Mr. and Mrs. Taylor. Probably as a hired hand. One thing about Jason really rankled, though. Most young, unmarried men noticed her, some even going out of their way to attract her attention. Jason seemed more interested in Karl.

Tommy stood. "Guess I'll head out for a while, too."

Mama watched Tommy walk away whistling. A frown creased lines between her eyes. "He must have a girl. Do you know, Katie?"

"Oh, don't worry, Mama. I saw him talking to a dainty, little thing with long, blond curls today. Amanda's her name. From what I saw, she's so silly. I don't see how he could get serious about her."

Chapter 5

Katie braced herself as the wagon bounced aboard the ferry. Rachel sat beside her while Daniel guided the oxen. Susanna snuggled close when she was thrown against Katie.

"I'm glad you decided to ride with us." Rachel smoothed her skirt over her bent knees. "Crossing the river is a little scary, isn't it?"

"More than a little." From her position behind the seat, Katie peered out at what she could see of the overcast sky and the river lapping against the ferry.

"I know, but we'll be all right. Daniel's a good driver. As soon as they get us secured, we only have to hang on while we float across."

"Where's Mama?" Susanna's small voice trembled.

Katie patted her arm. "You're fine. Mama, Dad, and Karl went on ahead of us. We can't see them right now, but they're already across the river. We'll be with them soon."

Susanna's lower lip stuck out, but only her large, blue eyes showed her fear.

Katie agreed with her. If she had her way, she'd be hiding under the covers until they arrived safely on the opposite bank.

Rachel leaned forward and looked out. "There are still some cattle in the water. I don't see Tommy or Jason. Weren't they going to ride your horses across with your cows?"

"Yes, but they went earlier, too. Maybe they're already across." Katie shivered. "I hope so."

She wrapped her hands around her upper arms and rubbed, trying to warm herself as an unreasonable fear seemed to grip her soul. This was their first big crossing. That had to be the reason she felt so uneasy. Maybe she and Susannah should have ridden with their parents. When Rachel asked her to ride with her and Daniel, she'd thought it sounded like fun. But it wasn't. Not much on this journey had been, and they'd scarcely gotten started on the long trail to Oregon.

Another jolt and the ferry reached the bank. Katie held Susanna close as Daniel shook the reins and called for the oxen to move out. "Get on there. Haw!"

With a jerk and shudder, the wagon creaked and bumped its way off the ferry.

"Where's my mama?" Susanna scowled at Katie. "I want my mama."

"I should've left you with her." Katie sniffed as the wagon came to a halt. "Come on, we'll go find Mama right away."

Rachel climbed from the wagon first. "There's a crowd gathering down by the bank. Maybe your folks are with them. I wonder what's going on."

Katie crawled out and helped Susanna down. She looked where Rachel pointed. Everyone seemed to be standing in a circle several yards downstream from where they were. She clasped her hands together and shivered from the breeze blowing off the river. Or from nerves. She wasn't sure which. "I hope nothing's happened. Maybe we should go see."

Katie took one of Susanna's hands while Rachel took the other, and they headed toward the group. Without warning the crowd parted, and Katie's parents appeared. Dad had his arm around Mama as if he were supporting her. Her head was bowed, and she stumbled.

Katie's heart wrenched within. "She's crying. Rachel, something's wrong."

Her feet wouldn't move. Rachel stopped, too, and looked back at her. Susanna looked up at Katie. Tears swam in her eyes. She jerked away. "I want my mama."

When Susanna's hand slipped from hers, Katie barely felt it. She watched through a haze as her little sister ran to their parents. Where was Tommy? And Karl? Maybe it was someone else. Even as the thought ran through her mind, she knew it was selfish, but she didn't care. She had to know. To quiet this fear that one of her brothers was hurt.

She broke into a run. Dad reached for her. "No, Katie,

don't go there."

She avoided his hand and pushed her way through those still standing in loose groups whispering or silent. Jason looked up from where he knelt on the ground. He stood and grabbed her shoulders. "No, Katie. I'm sorry."

She struggled against his restraining hands as she saw her little brother lying on the ground.

"Karl."

She called, but he didn't move. "Let me go, Jason. He's hurt. He needs help."

"He's gone, Katie." His voice choked. "Karl's gone."

"No-o-o." The word became a wail. She jerked from Jason, but her father caught her.

"It's too late, Katie. There's nothing we can do now." His strong arms imprisoned her with a gentle hug. "He wanted to help with the cows. I couldn't stop him. He jumped from the ferry when Calamity got caught in a whirlpool."

It couldn't be real. Through the tears that flooded her eyes, she watched anguish twist her mother's face. Mama's broken-hearted sobs made the ugly tragedy real. Even Dad poured out his grief in tears.

Jason turned away and knelt on the riverbank beside Karl, his face twisted, his head thrown back.

Katie reached for Susanna and held her tight as tears poured down both their cheeks. Only one in the family remained dry-eyed. Tommy stood slightly apart from the others staring woodenly at his little brother while a muscle twitched in his jaw.

Katie collapsed to the ground with Susanna. She held her little sister close and rocked back and forth while they cried. An arm slipped around her shoulders.

"Katie, I'm here to help." Rachel's soft voice penetrated the fog of Katie's mind.

Katie's eyes focused on Rachel, but she couldn't speak past the tears clogging her throat. Rachel's mother lifted Susanna from her lap.

"Lean on me." Rachel helped Katie. "You're coming with us. We've already talked to your folks and it's all right."

Katie turned toward her baby sister. Susanna snuggled against Mrs. Morgan's shoulder. Rachel led her away, but she couldn't go. Not yet. She turned back. "No, we can't leave him here. Not by himself."

Just then some men knelt on either side of Karl. Rachel's arm tightened around her. "He won't be alone. The men are taking care of him. Karl's in heaven with Jesus now. He'll never be alone again."

Rachel's soft voice soothed Katie so she finally allowed her friend to lead her toward the already forming night ring.

Susanna clung to Mrs. Morgan and soon went to sleep, but Katie sat and stared straight ahead, remembering and trying to forget. Rachel knelt beside her and placed her hand on Katie's shoulder. The love and concern in Rachel's brown eyes released the dam Katie had built against her tears. She fell into Rachel's arms and the two girls wept together, one in grief and one in compassion.

~*~

Jason stumbled back out of the way as the men took Karl. His mind whirled with scenes from the last few minutes, making no sense. Why couldn't they revive Karl? He was too young to die.

He lifted his face to the gray clouds and cried. "Lord, why are You doing this? He's only a child. His life has scarcely started. Take me instead, but please, let Karl live."

The men lifted Karl from the sand and carried him away. Jason wanted to follow, but he couldn't. He'd become more than an older friend to Karl when he led the little boy to accept the Lord the night before. His relationship had turned to that of a mentor, almost a parent. He cared about Karl and death had snatched him before he had a chance to grow.

Jason looked but couldn't find Tommy. Karl's parents followed the men carrying him away. Where were the girls? He swung around, wanting to be of use, but not knowing what else to do. Katie was with her friend from the wagon behind. Rachel and her mother had stepped in to care for both Katie and her little sister. There was nothing more he could do. He sank to the ground and bowed his head, letting the tears fall.

~*~

The wagon master held the train for the funeral early the next morning. Katie stood with her family only half listening to Mr. Taylor as he read the 23rd Psalm from his well-worn Bible. Everyone attended the services and grieved with the Donovans. Karl's death was the first in what they all feared might be many before they reached their destination.

Rachel stood with her family a few steps away. Jason was with an older woman Katie assumed was Mrs. Taylor. He lifted his head for a moment and met Katie's gaze. The anguish on his face brought fresh tears to her eyes, and she looked away, hurting for him and for herself.

Clay stood close behind Katie. Although he didn't touch her, she knew he was there and felt the warmth of his comforting presence.

Karl lay wrapped in a blanket on the ground beside a quickly dug grave in the middle of the trail. Katie couldn't bring herself to look at him. It wasn't real. He should get up and laugh at the joke he'd played on them. He wasn't really dead. He couldn't be.

Tears ran unceasingly down her cheeks. Her eyes burned from all she'd shed throughout the night, and the pain in her chest refused to go away.

She lifted her head and looked at Tommy. As much as she hurt, surely his pain must be even worse. Last night he disappeared until late in the night. Dad, already racked with grief, searched for him until he didn't know where else to look. They all stayed up until he stumbled into camp, reeking of alcohol, but with no explanation for his actions. He fell over a bucket and mumbled about growing up to be just like Dad. He was obviously trying to block out what had happened. He stood now with an expression as hard and unmoving as a stone. A muscle twitched in his jaw as if he were angry.

"Amazing Grace, how sweet the sound . . ."

The people sang with tears and concern in their eyes. Karl's death had brought the company closer together. Katie turned away before Dad dropped the first shovel of dirt into the shallow grave. She stumbled blindly and would have fallen except Clay's arm encircled her shoulders.

"Katie, are you all right?"

She swung toward him, glaring at him. "What do you think? My little brother's dead and my big brother doesn't care."

Clay stood silent a moment looking into her eyes. "Tommy cares all right."

She looked down, anger toward the injustice burning in her voice. "He got drunk last night, Clay. His brother not even in the grave yet and he goes out and gets drunk. Oh, yeah, he really cares, doesn't he?"

Clay's eyes narrowed. "Where did he get strong drink? It's supposed to be for medical purposes only."

Katie shrugged. "I don't know. I guess someone has some, and they let him have it."

"Well, they'd better keep it well hidden because the wagon master won't take kindly to anyone spreading alcohol around for anything other than medicine."

Katie looked at Clay, and her heart felt as if it weighed a ton. "You haven't understood a thing I said, have you?"

He frowned. "Of course. You're concerned about Tommy. I am, too."

Rachel spoke at her side. "Katie, is there anything I can do?"

Katie turned from Clay. She reached out, and Rachel embraced her. "I'm so sorry, Katie. I can't believe this has happened."

Tears sprang anew to Katie's aching eyes. "I know. This has to be a bad dream. Only I'm afraid I won't wake up from it."

Rachel pulled back and shook her head. "No, Katie, but it will get better with time. Just turn it over to Jesus, and He'll give you comfort."

Katie stared at her friend. Such useless words. Not that she blamed Rachel. She probably believed what she said.

~*~

Katie stayed in the wagon as mile after mile separated her from her little brother. Rachel said things would get better in time. If so, why did the hole in her heart grow larger with each mile they traveled? That night they made camp eighteen miles from Karl.

"Katie, can you milk Nanny?" Dad met her as she climbed from the wagon.

The nanny goat bleated same as she did every night when they stopped. Karl always milked her. Tears filled Katie's eyes, and a sob escaped.

"Oh, forget it." Dad turned toward the goat. "I'll do it."

Even Nanny missed Karl. Her bleats became a cry for the boy who had played with her while he milked her. Katie shrank from the sound, but couldn't get away. She had to help Mama fix supper. As if anyone would feel like eating.

Dad brought the milk to Mama. "I didn't get as much as—" He shrugged. "As usual. But here it is."

"Thank you." Mama held her head high when she took the milk although she didn't look at Dad.

"I hope we're not intruding." Mr. Bartlett, from the wagon in front of theirs, stepped into their camp. His wife stood beside him. "We just stopped by to tell you how sorry we are and to see if there's anything we can do for you folks."

"Thank you." Mama almost whispered the words.

Dad nodded. "We appreciate your offer, but we'll do all right. We have to."

"I understand." They turned as if to leave.

"There's one thing." Dad stopped them. "Would you be able to use a good milk goat?" He cleared his throat and motioned toward the goat. "Nanny was a pet of Karl's. Well, truthfully, he made pets out of all the animals, which is why he—"

Tears filled Katie's eyes. She couldn't bear hearing about Karl. She turned away and blocked Dad's voice out. Thankfully, the Bartletts didn't stay long and when they left, Nanny went with them.

Mama didn't seem to care. She looked one way and then another, past the wagons as if looking for someone. When they sat down to eat, and Tommy hadn't shown up, Katie understood she'd been looking for him. Neither Dad nor Mama mentioned his absence.

Katie forced a little food past the knot in her throat, although she hadn't felt like eating all day. Now she ate for Mama. Already dark circles framed Mama's eyes and her face was so pale. The shock of Karl's death could harm the baby. The unseen life her mother carried became even more important now. Katie felt so old and tired. Life seemed especially fragile. How easily and quickly it could be taken away.

~*~

After she ate, Katie took the bucket to a nearby stream to get water. When she returned, Jason Barnett sat visiting with her dad. She ignored them and began washing dishes.

"Katie, let me help." Mama's voice sounded soft by her side.

"No. You go sit down. You've done enough today. I'll get these clean and put away." Katie urged her mother to rest and was glad when she reluctantly turned back to sit by the men.

Katie worked quickly as she heard Karl's name mentioned again and again. How could they sit there and talk about him as if everything was all right? Her tears cooled the wash water and her heart became a leaden ball that bounced with each mention of his name. She wanted to scream.

Finally the dishes were done, and she walked past the others without looking their way.

Dad called out, reproach lining his voice. "Katie, we have company."

She spared him a glance. "No, Dad. You have company. I don't. You can talk about Karl all you want to because I won't stay here to hear it."

She didn't slow her steps, but before she left the circle of light from the campfire, she heard Jason's voice. "With your permission, Sir, I'll see that she's all right."

His footsteps sounded behind her, but she ignored them. Tears burned her eyes. She'd already cried a bushel of tears. There should be no more left. A short distance from camp she stopped and leaned against a tree in a dark place where no prying eyes could witness her misery.

A twig snapped, and she rolled her eyes. Who else but

Jason? Maybe if she ignored him, he'd leave. She looked up into the night sky at an especially bright star and fixed her gaze on it.

"Miss Donovan," Jason spoke softly. "Is there anything I can do for you?"

Katie whirled to face him. "Yes. You can tell me why God did this to us."

Jason's eyes widened as he stared at her. "I don't believe God did it."

"Well, He sure didn't stop it."

"No, but sometimes God allows things to happen and eventually good comes."

"Good!" Katie stared at him in disbelief. Her voice grew sarcastic. "Oh, sure, excuse me for forgetting all the good taking my brother has caused."

"Did you know Karl gave his life to God the night before he died?"

A sneer crossed Katie's face. "He told me. So how could a loving Heavenly Father take the life of a boy who had just given his life to Him? That doesn't seem loving to me."

The blue of Jason's eyes in the dim light of the moonlit night seemed black as he looked at Katie. He remained silent so long she wondered if he would answer. Strangely enough, she very much wanted him to.

In a soft voice, he finally spoke. "God's ways are so far above our ways that we can't always understand them. God sees the future while we only see the past and present and as the Bible says, even what's in front of our faces is only as clear as if we are looking through a dark glass."

Jason shuffle his foot through the leaves. "Karl is enjoying heaven right now because he became a Christian. I wouldn't want to take that away from him, and I don't think you would either. We don't know what might have happened in his future if he had lived. He might have drifted from God or something could have happened making his life miserable. We don't know. I do know God loves him, and He loves you, too."

In spite of her anger and fear, Jason's words spoke to her heart. All her life Katie had heard God loved her. Jason might be right, but knowing the truth did little to ease her pain. Her voice became a whisper as tears filled her throat. "I miss Karl so much. He was my little brother. He was so alive and now he's . . ."

A sob choked off the rest of her words. She buried her face in her hands as her shoulders shook.

His strong arms pulled her into his embrace. His warmth and strength surrounded her, seeping into her body, releasing tension while one hand gently rubbed a circle on the middle of her back. If only he could hold her forever. She didn't want to leave the first shelter she'd found since Karl died.

Chapter 6

*T*he days passed slowly without further incident. Firewood was plentiful and every few miles, the Kansas River showed up to supply water and remind Katie of her loss. She hated the river, yet it pulled at her emotions with a horrible fascination. Only when they veered away from the water, did her muscles relax. Then one night the tension returned when their train set up camp at the Vermillion River.

After supper, as the sun set the western sky aflame, Katie slipped away from her family. Three days passed, and still her heart hurt so much she could think of nothing but Karl. She wandered aimlessly through the company, speaking only when someone called a greeting. She came to the side of the large wagon circle nearest the Vermillion River as if drawn against her will.

She climbed over the chain and wagon tongue between two wagons and walked slowly toward the edge of the riverbank. With the train behind her, she stopped and stared at the water rushing downstream.

"What are you doing out here?" Jason touched her arm

She hadn't heard him approach, but she wasn't alarmed. To be frightened, one had to feel, and Katie wondered if she would ever feel again.

"I felt like walking." A faint smile crossed her lips as she turned to look up at him. "What are you doing out? More good deeds?"

"I thought you needed an escort." Jason's hand tightened on her arm. "In case you don't know, there are Kansa Indians living in these parts, and I've heard they're not the most civilized tribe."

"I wasn't thinking of Indians." Katie looked out over the

water at an enormous American Elm tree on the opposite bank. It stood tall and proud as a sentinel keeping watch over the river. Her gaze lowered to the ground at the foot of the tree and the drop off to the river below. A soft gasp escaped her lips.

Jason seemed to understand her fear. He touched her shoulder in a comforting gesture. "Don't worry. By tomorrow, we'll be across with no trouble."

"How?"

"We'll wrap chains around one of these trees and lower the wagons one at a time. It's been done before. I'm sure we'll have to again."

Don't worry? Of course she didn't worry. She didn't care anymore. She'd already cried all the care out of her heart. Drops fell on her crossed arms, telling her she was wrong. She swiped at her eyes and found a steady stream running down her cheeks. This wasn't fair. "Jason, why did he have to die?" She whispered. "I miss him. It hurts, Jason. It really hurts."

Katie turned so her forehead touched Jason's chest as he tightened his hold around her. Strength and comfort seeped into her emotions from his concern. He didn't answer, but held her until her crying slowed.

She must look awful. Her lashes were wet. Her eyes always got red when she cried. She covered her face, but the image in her mind didn't go away. Her face was probably blotchy, too. He shouldn't see her like this, but there was no place to hide.

He tucked a soft cloth in her hand. His handkerchief.

She repaired her face as much as she could before lifting her head. "I'm sorry. Crying on you is becoming a habit."

Jason loosened his hold without taking his arms away. "I don't mind. Thank you for calling me Jason."

Katie pulled away. "I'm sorry. I didn't realize I did."

He dropped his arms. "If you've seen enough of the river, we'd better get back. I didn't have time to bring my gun, and I wouldn't want to meet any Indians without it."

She walked beside him, her mind scarcely comprehending what had just happened. Little in her life now seemed real, as if a fog surrounded her. Jason had held her in his arms, and she'd found comfort there. He confused and frightened her, yet he seemed as a rock in his solid strength. He didn't approve of her, but he provided more comfort and understanding than anyone else had. Even more than Clay. His attempt at comfort had left her frustrated by his lack of understanding. Why couldn't Clay be more like Jason?

~*~

Jason kept a wary eye out for Indians, but didn't see anything. At least Katie hadn't wandered far from the wagons, but he didn't like the way she'd acted. As if she didn't care about herself. She showed no fear when he mentioned the danger she could have faced. Had Karl's death affected her deeper than he'd known? His heart ached for hers.

Lord, keep Katie in the palm of Your hand. Help her heal from her loss. Be with her entire family. Tommy also seems to be hurting beyond the range of Your comfort. If I can help them, please show me how.

Tonight, he would ask Ma and Pa Taylor to pray with him for the Donovan family.

Katie looked up at him with wide green eyes. "Thank you for being there. I don't know how you do it, but you always seem to know when I need help."

What would she say if she knew he couldn't seem to stay away from her? He didn't know what she did all the time, but as often as he could, he checked to see if she was all right. Not that he'd tell her that. Instead, he chuckled. "I happened to see you climb over the chains. Last I heard that was discouraged. You do know it's safer inside the circle of wagons, don't you?"

Her smile appeared sad. "Yes, I've heard that said a few times. I'm sorry. I never thought, but I'll try to from now on. I don't want to cause any more grief for my family."

"I'm glad to hear that." Jason touched her arm. "Here, let me help you over these chains."

Katie took his hand, warming his heart. He shouldn't feel this way. Her beliefs were different from his, or maybe she just hadn't realized yet what God had to offer. How much He loved her and cared about every part of her life. That He was waiting to heal her broken heart even now.

He released her hand when she seemed steady on her feet.

48

"Are you all right?"

She nodded. "I'll be fine. I'll return your handkerchief as soon as I've laundered it unless you need it back right away."

He fell into step with her as they walked back toward her parents' wagon. "No, that's fine."

She stopped in the shadows just before they reached the wagon and turned to look up at him. He let his gaze travel over her face and fought the urge to move closer.

She smiled. "Thank you. You've been such a help to my family. Even tonight when I went a little crazy."

"It's all right."

"But I'm sorry because I see the danger now, not just for me, but also to you. I shouldn't have walked out to the river. I don't know why I do things like that. Since Karl—I don't know, I just felt as if I had to see it. Sort of like I was drawn against my will. I'm sorry."

"It's not a problem, Katie." He stepped back. "Give yourself time to heal. Will you be all right now?"

All at once, Jason had to get away. If he didn't he'd pull Katie into his arms again and then where would he be?

At her nod, he turned and walked away. He needed to be careful or he'd give in to his feelings that were growing stronger with each encounter. Holding her close, comforting her, and feeling the tug of emotions her tears brought didn't help. Maybe he should keep his distance. No doubt he should, but could he? That was a question he couldn't answer.

~*~

That night Katie lay beside Susanna and stared into the darkness, the river filling her mind. Steep riverbanks towered above rapidly moving water. The thought of entering that rushing water sapped the strength from her muscles. Tomorrow, there'd be no ferry. Each wagon would be driven into the water to float across the river. The tremble deep inside wouldn't stop.

Sleep claimed her body, but her mind played out her fears as she fell into the river, caught in a strong whirlpool that pulled her ever downward. She fought against the twisting spiral to no avail. Water, darker than night, closed over her head. She threw her arms up reaching for someone or something solid to hold.

49

To pull her to safety.

"Katie. Katie." Someone called to her from the shore. "Katie, wake up."

She opened her eyes to see her mother leaning over her. "Wake up, Katie. You're having a bad dream."

A shudder coursed through her. "I was in the river."

Mama pushed Katie's hair back from her damp forehead. "No, you're right here safe. It's all right."

A tear ran down Katie's temple and another followed. "Mama, I'm so scared." Her voice shook. "I was in the river. Just like Karl. I couldn't swim. It sucked me under."

"No, sweetheart. It was just a dream. You are safe." Tears ran unchecked down Mama's face as she gathered Katie close.

Katie clung to her mother. "We can't get across this river. I know we can't. The bank is so steep. There's no ferry."

"I know, sweetheart. I know." Mama held her and talked softly, gently rocking her. "But we can cross it, and we will be all right. I have peace about this one."

Mama's soft voice had a soothing effect on Katie. "There will be many rivers to cross, and they won't be easy. But we will cross them one by one. God will be with us. I know you don't understand now, but He was with Karl. Never did God turn His back on Karl."

Mama sang softly in her sweet, clear voice. "Rock of Ages, cleft for me. Let me hide myself in Thee."

As her mother sang, Katie's fears dissolved leaving her sleepy. When the song ended, Katie lay back down. "I'm sorry, Mama. I didn't mean to wake you. I'll be fine now. Thank you."

Mama patted Katie's shoulder before going back to her own mattress.

~*~

Katie awoke the next morning while it was still dark. The buzz of activity in camp stirred her unrest. Mama's confidence in their safety soothed her fears, but didn't remove them. She stood near the edge of the bank and watched their wagon as it slid downward toward the river. What kept it from flipping end over end as it slowly made the descent remained a mystery.

She helped Susanna and Mama slide down the steep bank

to the wagon below. When they climbed in, Katie lay down on her mattress and pulled her quilt above her head. The porous cloth couldn't protect her from the river, but it made her feel better. Being unable to see what was going on helped calmed her fears.

A sudden jerk and splash let her know they were in the water. Her heart raced as she visualized them being swept downstream. She pulled the cover closer and squeezed her eyes closed.

The scraping sound of wood on rocks and a sudden jolt brought her straight up expecting the wagon to roll. She cried out. "Oh!"

"Katie, you can wake up now." Susanna tapped on her arm. "Mama says we're here."

Katie swung toward her baby sister and tossed the quilt aside. Susanna stood beside her with wide blue eyes filled with concern. Katie opened her arms. "I could use a big hug. How about you?"

Susanna grinned and leapt into Katie's arms. Katie lifted her to the bed. As small arms circled her neck, giddy relief washed over her, and she laughed. How foolish she was. Even Suzy was braver than her. She nuzzled the soft baby hair against her cheek. "I saw a big tree over on this side. How would you like to see if we can find it now?"

Susanna nodded and struggled to free herself. Katie looked over her head at their mother and shared a smile. She gave Suzy one last, quick hug before releasing her, then followed her from the wagon.

The tree was big and old; it had surely seen at least a hundred seasons of new growth such as this one. Katie stood with Susanna under the overspreading branches and lifted her face to look all the way to the top. Something about the tree gave Katie a sense of peace. Surely its old age indicated that life would go on. They'd successfully crossed the river, and Katie felt as if she'd conquered an unseen foe.

~*~

That night after the evening meal Clay crouched beside Katie as she sat on the ground leaning against a wagon wheel.

"Will you walk with me? We'll stay inside the night ring."

"Yes, if Dad says it's all right." She had nothing else to do and being with Clay might ease the heaviness in her heart that never seemed to go completely away.

With her father's permission, they set out. Their steps slowed, keeping time with the mournful song of the violin coming from one of the campsites. Katie identified with its mood.

Clay took Katie's hand in his, interlocking their fingers. He moved just outside the light of the campfires. A thrill at his daring raced through her veins.

He gave her a searching look. "How are you feeling now? I mean, I know it was hard on you—losing your brother and all."

She looked away. He couldn't know how hard. "It has been hard. Time will ease the hurt. At least that's what everyone says."

"Yeah, I guess so." He cleared his throat. "We've got a good start. On the trail, I mean. It'll still be a long time before we get there, though."

"Six months." Katie spoke into the gathering darkness. "It will take all summer. A lot can happen in that length of time."

"I suppose." He stopped so they stayed in the shadows between campfires. "I know one thing I want to happen."

Katie's heart raced at his nearness, the way he pulled her closer. In the dark, she barely made out his hesitant smile. "Do you remember what I told you the night of the dance?"

Katie nodded. "I think so."

"I said I intended to win your heart before we reach Oregon. Katie, I wasn't joking. Lumber is big in Oregon. I have plans. I want to find some land that has plenty of good trees on it. I want to build a mill and go into business. I enjoy working with wood. My father's a carpenter. I've helped him all my life. I'm young, but that means I have plenty of time to build a good business."

Katie listened, but where did she fit in? Almost every sentence he uttered began with the word "I" while he said nothing about her part in his life. He knew what he wanted, and he'd probably accomplish what he set out to do. But she didn't want to risk her heart where there was no heart given in return. He kept her hand clasped in his, but he seemed unaware of her presence.

"Clay."

He cut off mid-sentence and looked at her.

"I need to get back to camp now."

"Oh, sure." He started walking again. "Yep, Oregon is the place to go. If not a mill, I could become a carpenter. They'll be a lot of building going on there. New towns springing up all over, I'd wager."

Katie sighed.

~*~

Less than a week later near Little Blue River, Katie sank to the grass beside a sparkling stream in a refreshing green valley. A waterfall cascaded several feet from a ledge of rocks into the water, creating a feeling of peace and rest.

Rachel settled beside her.

"I think I could stay here forever." Katie spoke in hushed tones in keeping with her feelings.

"I know." Rachel's dark brown eyes sparkled as she looked around. "Don't you wish we could camp like this every night?" She leaned forward to dip her hand in the water, then scooped some up and drank it.

"Is it good?"

"M-m-m. It's delicious. So cold, like it has ice in it. Get some for yourself. I'm going to fill my bucket."

Katie drank her fill and leaned back on her hands. "I really do think I could stay here forever. Who needs Oregon?"

Rachel smiled. "It's beautiful here, but this is wild country. Indians live around here. We need more than beauty in our lives, I guess. Are you ready to go back?"

Katie gave a discontented sigh as she pulled herself away with one last look at the waterfall. Oregon probably wouldn't be half this pretty. She turned away and walked back to camp with Rachel.

That night violin music sounded, playing a lively song. Soon the strains of a guitar joined and then another. Katie's toes tapped in time as she washed dishes. She put the last one away and watched as people began moving toward the center of the night ring where someone had built a large fire for light. As couples walked by she watched for Clay. Surely he would come to take her to the dance.

Tommy stepped down from the wagon buttoning a clean shirt. "You still here with that music going on?"

Katie made a face at him. "Someone had to wash dishes."

"Not me. I'm heading over to see if Amanda wants to do some foot stompin' with me."

"Hey, what happened to taking your little sister to the dance?" Katie pouted.

Tommy grinned. "Trust me, sis, it just isn't the same thing." He sobered then. "Besides, you might want to take a look at Mama. She's lying down in the wagon. She said it was just a headache, but. . ."

He looked toward the crowd of people and frowned. "So much for that. Here comes your escort. I'll get out of your way."

He turned and quickly stepped over the wagon tongue to the outside of the ring of wagons. When he disappeared behind their wagon, Katie shook her head. What was wrong with Tommy? Did he dislike Clay so much he would go out of the way to avoid him?

She glanced back at Clay. He stopped to talk to a man. She smoothed her apron then touched her tousled hair. She must look a fright.

A quick glance at Susanna sitting on the ground listening to the music assured her she was all right. If she hurried, she'd have time to comb her hair before Clay reached the wagon. She climbed inside and almost stumbled over her mother.

"Mama, what is wrong?" She knelt beside the mattress and touched the back of her hand to her mother's forehead.

Mama smiled and caught Katie's hand in hers. "There's no fever. It's just a silly, old sick headache. I thought it would go away if I rested a while."

"Mama, where is Dad?"

Her mother pressed her fingertips against her head. "On guard duty."

Katie looked out the end of the wagon. Clay would be there any minute. "Tommy just left. Someone needs to stay and help you with Suzy."

"Katie." Clay stood outside the end of the wagon.

She stuck her head out. "I'll be there in a minute, Clay."

Mama patted Katie's arm when she turned back around. "Go on, Katie, and visit with your young man. I'll be fine. Just tell Suzy to come in the wagon so I'll know where she is."

Suzy would never be content to sit in a wagon with the excitement of the music and dancing going on outside. Trying to keep her there would only make Mama feel worse. With a leaden heart, Katie climbed from the wagon.

Clay's dark brown eyes lit up at the sight of her. A smile slowly crossed his handsome face. "I'll never understand why a pretty gal like you has to spend so much time primping. Now I'll have to fight off all the other guys." His voice dropped as he slipped an arm around her waist. "Maybe we'd better get married now so everyone will know who you belong to. Come on, that music won't last all night."

Katie's emotions churned between Clay's smooth talk and her responsibility toward her mother. She allowed him to pull her several steps away from their camp before reality found place in her mind. Mama needed her. If Clay meant what he said, he'd stay with her.

She stopped walking, jerking Clay to a halt. "I can't go, Clay. Mama's sick, and she needs someone to watch Suzy."

Clay looked back at Susanna sitting on the ground with her rag doll. "She looks fine to me. Why can't your dad or Tommy watch her?"

"They aren't here." She looked at him. "Why don't you stay with me?"

"You want me to babysit your little sister?" His voice held a note of disbelief. "Come on, Katie. There's a dance going on. You don't want to stay here anymore than I do. We work hard and now's our chance to have fun. There may not be another opportunity like this before we get to Oregon. Now come on. Let's go."

Clay grabbed Katie's arm and pulled her forward.

Katie jerked away. "Don't pull me, Clay. I said I wasn't going. If you don't want to stay with me, go by yourself."

"Oh, trust me, I won't be by myself long." Clay's jaw clenched.

Katie's eyes burned, but she refused to give in to either him or the weakness of crying. "Fine, Clay. Go and find someone else to build your lumber empire with. I'll sit here with Suzy and feel sorry for whoever is stupid enough to listen to you and your flattery."

Before Clay could respond, Katie swung away, stomped the short distance to Susanna and sat on the ground. She kept her back toward Clay as she fought the burning in her eyes.

When she finally turned to look, he was gone. The next wagon over belonged to the Morgans. Rachel's mother sat alone in one of three chairs just outside the wagons.

Katie concentrated on her neighbors rather than think about Clay. It must be nice having two wagons. Chairs were a luxury when you could sit on the ground, she supposed, but it would be nice to have more than one chair.

Rachel came from between the two wagons and approached her mother. They spoke then she crossed the ground to Katie.

"Hi. May I sit with you?"

Katie nodded. "Sure. Suzy and I are listening to the pretty music."

"It is pretty, isn't it?" Rachel sat down and gave a quick laugh. "You will never guess what I just did."

Katie smiled. "Probably not."

Rachel looked at Katie and grimaced. "I threw water on your brother."

"You what?"

"Honest, I did." Rachel buried her face in her hands. Her cheeks were two spots of red when she looked up. "My father asked me to throw some wash water out so I carried it to the outer side of the wagons and tossed it. I didn't think about anyone being there."

Katie laughed. "Tommy went that way to avoid Clay. I wish I could have seen it. I'll bet he was surprised." Then she sobered. "I wonder why he didn't come back and change. He was going to take Amanda to the dance."

Rachel nodded. "I know. I watched him go get her."

Katie recognized the longing in Rachel's voice. So her friend really did have feelings for Tommy. She liked Rachel. It would be fun having her for a sister-in-law. All she needed to do was convince Tommy. She smiled at the thought, knowing her brother would rebel at the first sign of her matching him with anyone, let alone one of her friends.

"So he went to the dance all wet, huh?"

"No." Rachel shook her head. "Just his boots were wet."

"Too bad." Katie laughed again. "I wish you'd drenched him.

Rachel smiled.

"Would it be asking too much if I leave Suzy with you while I run to the wagon to check on my mother?"

"Of course not. What's wrong?"

"She has a headache. I shouldn't take long."

Katie climbed into the wagon and found her mother sleeping, so she didn't disturb her. She backed out of the wagon and jumped nimbly to the ground. Male laughter came from where she'd left Rachel and Susanna. She swung to look.

Jason Barnett. Her eyes focused on the dark form kneeling in front of Rachel. They seemed deep in conversation and didn't notice her. She watched the firelight play across Jason's golden-blond hair. Rachel laughed at something Jason said, and his deeper voice joined her merriment. A sharp twinge shot through Katie's heart surprising her. Rachel deserved Jason. He seemed to be a very nice man. So nice, in fact, she'd do well to forget Tommy.

Katie forced a smile and walked the short distance to join them.

Jason looked up at her approach. "Well, hi. I thought you'd be at the dance."

So he really was here to see Rachel. Again that sharp twinge annoyed her. She shrugged. "Oh, I didn't want to go."

Concern darkened the blue in his eyes as he searched her face. "I'm glad."

Clay's rejection seemed unimportant as Katie tried to read the meaning behind Jason's softly spoken words. Why would he care if she stayed or went to the dance? After all, he'd come to visit with Rachel, hadn't he?

Chapter 7

"*C*an you believe we're picking these up?" Katie wrinkled her nose and held up a dried buffalo chip.

Rachel laughed. "No, but we should be thankful God has given us fuel to pick up. Who'd have thought there'd be no wood here? The trees were plentiful not that many miles back."

"I know." Katie stuffed the chip with the others in the bag and looked around. Not a tree stood within sight in any direction.

The country they'd entered was a dry, sandy land. Sagebrush squatted where trees should be standing and signs of buffalo were seen all around. Katie didn't mind picking up the dried chips, but the thought of what she carried was less than appealing. She would appreciate them that evening when the time came to build a campfire, though. After all, they did make a good fire.

Jason rode up on Star beside the girls and stopped. He leaned slightly toward them and lifted his hat. "Hello, ladies. I see you've developed an attraction to what even the buffalo didn't want."

He shook his head in mock amazement, a grin on his face.

Katie glared at him, but Rachel laughed. "This is one attraction I hope I don't have to continue for long."

Jason chuckled and turned his attention to Katie. "Your brother asked me to deliver a message to you. Some of the men are getting up a hunting party and he wants to go. Would you be willing to drive the cows while he's gone?"

"Of course, I'll do what I can to help." Katie's gaze shifted to the horse Jason rode. "Are you going on the hunt, also?"

"I planned to." Jason hesitated. "Tommy said I could borrow Star. But you'll need her for the cattle, won't you?"

"Oh, no. I can walk behind a bunch of cows as easily as I can walk through a bunch of buffalo chips."

Jason frowned. "Are you sure?"

"Yes, I'm sure." Katie waved away his concern.

Rachel spoke up. "Let's deposit our fuel in the wagons, and I'll walk with you."

"Okay." Katie looked up at Jason. "Tell Tommy we'll be along shortly."

Jason nodded and rode on.

"I think Jason cares for you."

Katie looked at Rachel. "And I'm sure you are wrong. Jason is much more suitable for you. Didn't you notice the way he kept looking at you?"

"Me?" Rachel's dark eyes grew large. "He was looking at you."

Katie laughed. "Poor Jason. Neither of us want him so we're passing him back and forth like a hot potato. What a shame! He really is such a nice man."

The girls separated at the wagons to deposit their fuel then met a few minutes later to walk the short distance where Tommy and Jason waited for them with the cattle.

Tommy grinned at Katie from the back of his horse. "Thanks, sis, I owe you one."

"Make sure you bring back something good to eat then."

Tommy nodded. "Yes, ma'am."

He looked at Rachel and his grin widened. "Hello, Miss Morgan. I didn't recognize you at first with no water."

Rachel's cheeks grew rosy, but she met his gaze with a smile. "Oh, I only carry water for protection at night. I didn't think there'd be a need for it today."

Tommy's laugh rang out. "In that case, I'll be careful to not sneak up on you again, especially at night." He turned his large black horse to the side. "I'd better be going or I'll miss the party. You girls enjoy yourselves."

Jason smiled at both Rachel and Katie before lifting his hand in a salute. He nudged Star forward at the same time Tommy urged Midnight into a gallop and both rode off to join the other men gathering on a nearby knoll.

~*~

That night after the supper dishes had been put away, Katie leaned back against the wagon wheel and looked at the velvety-black sky studded with a thousand twinkling stars. A slight breeze ruffled her hair. The nights were warmer now. She lifted her face and closed her eyes while the wind caressed her cheeks. Her leg muscles ached after herding the cattle all afternoon. She tried to rest, but her mind returned to the conversation she'd had with Rachel. Was Jason really attracted to her? If so, he didn't act like it. Before she could decide, she heard footsteps coming toward her. She watched in that direction, thinking it was her parents coming back from their visit with the Bartletts.

Tommy and Jason stepped out of the shadows and sank to the ground beside her.

"Have any trouble with the cows?" Tommy asked.

Katie shook her head. "No, Rachel helped me."

"Good." Tommy picked up a rock and tossed it up a couple of inches and caught it. "Say, sis, do you think you could take over the job with the cattle? I'd like to get back to scouting. Jeb asked me today if I was coming back."

Jason spoke then. "It will be easier with Star. I shouldn't have kept her today."

Katie turned and met his gaze. "That's fine. It is easier on horseback, but it's more lonesome. That's one reason I'm not looking forward to it. I don't mind the work, but I'll miss Rachel. She's a wonderful friend."

"Yes, she seems like a nice girl." Jason started to say more when someone stepped into the circle of their campfire.

Clay stood before them with his head bowed. He looked at Katie. "Would you go for a walk with me?" His voice sounded unsure.

Katie didn't want to forgive so quickly. "I thought you were mad at me."

Clay hesitated as he glanced toward Tommy and Jason. "I was wrong, Katie, but I don't want to talk about it here."

One look at her brother's frown and Jason's matching glare, and she understood his reasoning.

"Please, come walk with me."

Katie stood, but Tommy caught her hand. "I think you should stay here. We were talking."

She looked at Jason. He seemed especially interested in a rock he held in his hand. As Tommy had done earlier, he tossed it in the air and caught it. He obviously didn't care whether she went or stayed.

She shook Tommy's hand off. "I won't be gone long. You can visit with Jason."

She took Clay's arm and as soon as they walked out of the light she looked back. Both Tommy and Jason watched her with matching frowns. She ignored them. It was none of their business what she did.

~*~

Jason looked at the rock in his hand. The urge to see how far he could throw it surprised him. What did Katie see in Monroe? Good looks? He seemed to be a decent sort, but still something about the way he took possession of Katie bothered Jason. He glanced over his shoulder, but already the darkness had swallowed Katie from his sight. Maybe he should take a walk, just to make sure she was all right. He shifted, but stopped at Tommy's voice.

"Maybe I shouldn't be asking Katie to help with the cattle."

Jason focused on Tommy. Pulling his mind back from Katie wasn't easy. "Will she be all right?"

Tommy grinned. "When? Tonight or tomorrow on Star?"

Warmth crept up Jason's neck, and he hoped it didn't show. His lips curved. "I'll admit I don't trust Monroe as much as I'd like to, but I don't think he'd do anything to hurt a girl. He seems a good enough fellow. No, I meant riding herd on the cattle."

Tommy shrugged. "She did her share back home. Katie's used to hard work. Tending cattle can be dangerous, but I'm not worried about that. It's just—"

When Tommy looked away and clenched his jaw, Jason waited and breathed a prayer for his friend. If he had something to say, he'd say it in his own time.

After a moment, Tommy shrugged and turned back. He

spoke in a low voice. "I still can't believe Karl's gone. He loved those animals. Star was his horse, although Katie rode him sometimes, too. I get so angry when I think about what happened. Mama taught us to believe in God. She says Karl's with Him now. I'm not sure what to believe."

Jason held his breath. No words of condolence came to mind.

"At first I thought about turning against everything I've ever been taught. I got drunk the night after it happened." Tommy looked at Jason as if he expected a response. Maybe a rebuke.

Jason nodded.

Tommy picked up the rock he'd been playing with earlier and held it, looking at it. "Figured I might as well become like my dad, so I found a bottle. The funny thing is Dad hasn't taken a drink since the night he almost killed a man."

A harsh laugh escaped Tommy, and he tossed the rock and caught it. "I puked my insides out that night. Don't reckon I'll do any more drinking, either. At least, Mama will be happy about that. Too bad that's all she'll be happy about, though, because I don't intend to waste any more time talking to God. Karl's gone. Even God can't change that."

"I'm sorry, Tommy." A lump in Jason's throat blocked his words. He didn't know what he could say to help change anything, anyway. Sounded like Tommy's mind was made up. But Jason still talked to God, and he had no intention of quitting. In fact, he'd be doing even more praying now for both Tommy and Katie. They were hurting. They needed God more than they knew.

~*~

Clay kept just outside the light from campfires, but well away from the cattle corralled in the center of the ring of wagons. His hand closed over Katie's. "I'm sorry for the way I acted before. You know I didn't mean all the things I said."

"Then you shouldn't have said them." She didn't feel like forgiving him just yet.

"I couldn't help it. I got angry because I love you, Katie, and you acted like you didn't care."

Katie felt her heart melt. What was it about Clay Monroe that attracted her? She should turn from him, yet she felt captive in spite of herself. He was the best looking man she had ever seen, but he was also the most arrogant. Was he really sorry or had he just decided to renew his efforts to win her hand?

"My mother was sick. What did you expect me to do? If you love me the way you say you do, you would have stayed with me."

"I do love you, Katie. I want us to be married." Clay stopped and pulled Katie close. His head lowered and she felt powerless to resist as his lips touched hers in a brief kiss. Katie's heart pounded in her ears.

Clay claimed her lips again. This time the kiss deepened and Katie knew she must resist. This was not right. She did not belong to Clay. They were not betrothed. She made a feeble effort to push him away when a piercing scream split the muted night sounds.

Clay's head jerked up. He took Katie's hand to pull her with him. They followed others toward the screaming that continued to come from a wagon across the ring. Then, as quickly as it started, the screaming stopped.

"That's our wagon." Clay's voice choked.

Katie's heart sank. Already people were gathering around the wagon. Clay elbowed his way through the crowd, pulling Katie with him. The sight that greeted them nauseated Katie.

Clay's little sister, Mary Beth, lay on the ground, her legs exposed where her skirts had been burned away. They were an angry red, and blisters had already started forming on both legs from the ankles up as far as Katie could see.

Clay knelt beside his mother who cradled his sister's head in her lap while the doctor tended to her legs. Those standing nearby talked in hushed tones as they watched.

"She was playing tag with some other children." One woman spoke to another. "She tripped over a rock and stumbled into the campfire."

Katie pieced the story together from the whispered comments. When Mary Beth's skirt caught on fire she ran, frightened and screaming, to get away from the greedy flames licking at her dress and legs. The screaming had stopped when she passed out from shock and pain.

Doctor Clark finished bandaging her legs and looked at her parents. "Bad as it may look, it's not a deep burn. She's coming around now and will be in a lot of pain. While you carry her into your wagon, I'll go get something to ease the pain and help cure the burns."

When he hurried away, Clay picked up his sister. "I've got her, Dad."

His father nodded. "All right, Son. I'll climb into the wagon and you hand her to me."

Katie stood alone while the Monroe family took care of Mary Beth. Realizing there was nothing they could do, those who had gathered began to leave. The doctor returned and went into the wagon. Clay still didn't come out. Katie turned to leave and almost ran into Jason.

"Oh, I'm sorry." She stepped back.

He smiled down at her. "Don't be."

Tommy elbowed him. "Come on. Let's go back to our wagon."

They fell into place on either side of her. She felt bewildered, confused by what had happened. Poor Clay. He wouldn't even know she was gone. His mind was on his sister now.

That night Katie turned from one side to another on her narrow bed. The events of the day filled her mind in a jumble of thoughts. It seemed ages since she'd crawled from bed that morning. Clay said he loved her, but she was unsure of her feelings for him. Rachel said Jason cared for her, but he didn't act like it. And poor Mary Beth. The doctor said she stood a good chance of recovery, but she must be in so much pain. Katie finally fell asleep, and her dreams were as confused as her thoughts had been earlier.

Chapter 8

*O*ne evening in late June, the Morgan family joined the Donovan's for supper. Dad scraped the last morsel from his plate, then turned to Mr. Morgan. "We'll be slowed down again before long. The South Fork of the Platte River is just ahead. Should reach it in a day or two."

Mr. Morgan nodded. "I've heard the river is wide and shallow with a swift current."

"It's a mile wide, a foot deep, and useless."

Katie looked up at her father's words. As they'd traveled through the dry, sandy countryside, water had become more valuable than she'd ever dreamed possible. She spoke before she thought. "How can water be useless?"

Dad grinned. "Oh, water can be useless, Katie-girl. The Platte is alkaline. We can't drink it or we'll get sick. The animals, too. It's too muddy to wash in. Can't get much more useless than that."

Mr. Morgan agreed. "They say it's too thick to drink and too thin to plow."

The next morning Katie saw what they meant. The Platte looked more like flooded ground than a river. However, she was glad when they were safely across the shallow river as the current was much stronger than she had expected.

That evening Clay stopped by the wagon for the first time since his sister's accident. Instead of going for a walk, he seemed content to sit on the ground and lean against the wagon wheel with Katie.

"How's Mary Beth?"

Clay shrugged. "She's better, I think. She still hurts a great deal, though, and she isn't able to be up and about."

Clay seemed different somehow. Gone was the arrogance

and sense of excitement that Katie had found irresistible. She wasn't sure she liked the change. No doubt his mind remained with his little sister. In time he would likely return to normal. They talked for a while and he left before Katie expected him to, saying he should stay close to the wagon in case his parents needed him.

~*~

A few days later, when Tommy returned early from scouting, he relieved Katie from her job with the cows. She hadn't seen Rachel for a few days so she went in search of her. Rachel's brother, Daniel, saw Katie coming and called over his shoulder. "Hey, Rachel, your friend's here."

Katie kept pace with the wagons. She wiped a sleeve across her face, streaking dirt on the material as she did. She frowned at the smear she'd have to wash out. Would she ever be clean again? She was hot and tired. Dust kicked up by the animals stuck to whatever it landed on, including her face. A cool swim in a clear pond would be a real treat, but an impossibility in this dry land.

Rachel hopped from the wagon and joined her.

Katie shook her head at her friend. "You know, jumping from a moving wagon is not the safest thing you can do."

Rachel smiled and nodded. "I know, but I believe I've seen you do it before, too."

Katie shrugged. "I have, but not recently. I decided it wasn't a good example for Susanna."

"Where is Suzy?" Rachel looked toward the Donovan wagon and her eyes grew wide. "Oh, no."

"Taking a nap in the back of the—" Katie followed Rachel's line of vision and gasped. "No!" She screamed. "No, Suzy, don't."

Katie ran toward the wagon, yelling for Susanna to stay inside. But even as she ran, Susanna climbed from the back and stood hanging at the end of the wagon. Katie saw her face scrunched in fear as she wailed, too afraid to either let go and jump as she had seen Katie do or climb back inside.

Katie yelled for her father who drove the wagon, but knew he couldn't hear her any more than he could hear Susanna over the noise of more than a hundred oxen and almost as many wagons. Someone brushed past Katie as she ran and she saw Jason reach the wagon and Susanna. The relief of knowing he was there taking care of them brought weakness to her limbs, and she stumbled and fell several feet from the line of moving wagons.

"She's all right now." Rachel knelt beside Katie. "Did you get hurt when you fell?"

Katie shook her head. "No, I'm fine." Her breath came in short gasps. She watched Jason carry Susanna toward her.

Susanna reached for Katie as they got close, and Jason set her down. Katie pulled her into her arms and cried as she buried her face in her little sister's soft neck. Susanna's tears mixed with hers.

The little girl pulled back and patted her sister's face. "I'm sorry, Katie. I won't do that ever again."

"Susanna, I told you not to unless me or Tommy help you. You knew better. You could have been killed."

Fresh tears gathered in Susanna's large brown eyes. "I know, Katie. I was scared. Jason gotted me."

Katie took Jason's offered hand and stood, setting Susanna beside her. They all began walking as she held Susanna's hand. Susanna clung to Jason with her other hand.

Katie looked up at Jason. "How do you do that?"

He frowned. "Do what?"

"Show up every time I need you." Of course, there was the fire he built without her permission and the time Nanny butted her. She wrinkled her nose. "And sometimes when I don't."

Jason threw back his head and laughed. He pointed to the side. "Mr. and Mrs. Taylor's wagon is in the line next to yours. I saw what was happening, handed the reins to Mr. Taylor, and ran as fast as I could."

"Oh." Katie hadn't known where his wagon was. She liked the idea of him being close by. "I guess we should be thankful you can run fast."

Jason laughed again.

~*~

"Ash Hollow." Katie stood in the middle of the beautiful

68

oasis in such a barren countryside. The name didn't seem to fit as nothing she saw reminded her of ashes. When they stopped early in the day she found waving green grass as far as she could see, cedar trees in clusters dotted the countryside, and clear, sparkling streams of good water to drink and bathe in. The name didn't matter. She took a deep breath. Finally, she would get the bath she had craved for so long.

Katie ran toward the wagon next to theirs to find Rachel. They met halfway. "Will you go with me to the stream?"

"Of course." Rachel turned back calling over her shoulder as she walked away. "I'll get the things I need and meet you at your wagon."

Katie ran back to find her mother getting Suzy ready to joined several other girls and women who were as eager to soak in the clear water as they were. Katie grabbed what she needed and fell into step with Rachel. They found a quiet spot a short way from camp and, leaving their outer clothes hanging on nearby bushes, slipped into the refreshing water.

Some swam in small circles, while a few women washed quickly and climbed from the water almost as soon as they stepped in. Katie sank beneath the cleansing, cool waves while weeks of grime and dust floated off and away. She laid her head back soaking her long hair. "Oh, this feels so good."

"Turn around and I'll wash your hair, then you can wash mine." Rachel tugged on her shoulder until she obeyed.

Rachel's fingers massaging her scalp was so relaxing, she didn't even mind the tickle against her legs and feet as small fish swam past.

After the older women and young children went back, several of the young women stayed to enjoy the water as long as they could. The girls released emotions that had been suppressed on the hard trail and acted silly as they played in the water. They giggled and splashed while they bathed and washed their hair. Finally, in groups of two or three, they pulled themselves from the creek and dressed. Several had already started back when Katie and Rachel climbed the bank of the stream.

Katie dressed then slipped on her shoes. She bent over to

tie the laces when she felt a touch on her arm.

"Finish tying your shoe, but do it quickly." Rachel's voice came out in a hoarse whisper.

"What is it, Rachel?"

"Indians are watching us."

Weakness poured through Katie as the blood drained from her face. She couldn't faint! Just the thought of what would happen if she did caused her to panic even more. Then Rachel's quiet voice calmed her fears.

"We'll be all right. God is with us. If we walk back quietly, I don't think they will follow us. Help me tell the others. I doubt the Indians can understand our language."

With something to do, Katie felt better. She and Rachel moved through the girls and told them to walk back to camp as quickly as possible without acting frightened. Most of the girls did as they were told. A few at a time started the walk back to the wagons and safety.

Rachel spoke to Tommy's friend, Amanda, who had been combing her long, blond hair without paying attention to the others. Before Rachel could stop her, Amanda whirled toward the opposite bank, her eyes wide with fright. Her hand flew to her mouth and a piercing scream erupted.

Katie stared at Rachel while her heart almost stopped before taking off as fast as Amanda, who ran toward camp screaming all the way.

What could they do? There was no reason to act brave now. A splash behind them spurred Katie into motion as she grabbed Rachel's hand and ran after Amanda.

Whoops filled the air.

Katie didn't dare look behind. The Indians were gaining. She was sure she felt their breath and the brush of their hands reaching for her, yet how could they possibly have crossed the stream and climbed the bank so quickly?

~*~

Jason turned the oxen into the makeshift pen for the animals. They'd done a good job of pulling the Taylor's wagon all this way. He looked at the lush grass in the valley and breathed in the welcome scent of pine and fresh air. If only it would be like this the rest of the way to Oregon. The land they'd traveled through was fickle—never staying the same. The occasional oasis such as this one gave hope for a similar home at the end of the trail.

"Might as well enjoy it while we can." He spoke to himself and started back toward the wagon when a scream came from the direction the girls had gone earlier.

Katie! She'd been with them. His heart leapt and pounded as he took off running toward the screams that didn't stop. Other men joined his race toward the stream. He met the first group of women, but Katie wasn't with them.

"What's wrong?" He shouted out.

"Indians." The one word brought terror to his already frightened heart. He didn't have his rifle. He'd be no help, but he wouldn't return without Katie.

One girl ran toward him screaming. Then he saw the Indians. Three youth, who appeared to be barely in their teens, stopped chasing the girls and fled. He saw Katie with Rachel and his fear left as he slowed to a walk. The danger was over this time.

~*~

Katie's breath came in short pants more from fright than the run. Her heart pounded against her chest as if it would burst. Through a haze, she saw Amanda a few steps ahead, then men from camp ran toward them, rifles in hand.

Her confidence restored by the presence of the men, Katie glanced behind her and was amazed to see grins on the Indians' faces that quickly faded when they saw the men. With one last yell, all three young Indians turned and ran back the way they had come.

Katie slowed her pace to a walk. Her lungs burned with each intake of air. She and Rachel walked together, gasping for each breath.

Amanda flew toward Tommy and fell into his arms. She clung to him crying. Katie winkled her nose in disgust when he put his arm around her and led her back to camp while he talked in low tones. She glanced at Rachel and saw that she, too, had witnessed the exchange.

"You like Tommy, don't you?"

Rachel glanced quickly at Katie. "Of course, I like him."

Katie shook her head. "No, I mean you really like him."

"I know what you mean." Rachel's voice was so low Katie had to listen carefully. "But it doesn't matter how I feel. I'm a Christian, and I don't think Tommy is serving the Lord."

"What difference does that make?"

Rachel sighed. "God's word tells us that if two oxen are unequally matched they will be unable to pull together. It's the same with people. We should marry someone of like faith. My faith is more important to me than anything."

"Even the man you love?"

Rachel looked at Katie and nodded. "Yes, even the man I love."

So, she did love Tommy. A flash of anger toward her brother hit Katie. If he would just grow up and do the things he should, he could have Rachel. She was so much nicer then Amanda ever would be. Definitely a lot smarter.

Rachel's father held her in a close hug before walking away with his arm around her shoulders. Katie's father and Jason met her together.

"Can you tell us what happened?" Jason looked into her eyes.

She thought of the three Indians running behind her with silly grins on their faces. "I don't think those Indians were trying to catch us. I think they were just big boys playing a prank. They were trying to scare us because they thought it was funny."

Jason lifted his eyebrows. "Did their prank work?"

Katie nodded. "Oh, yes. I don't think I've ever been so scared in my life."

Chapter 9

*K*atie pulled her bonnet further forward. Maybe walking the short distance to look at a rock wasn't such a good idea. Not even one with a name like Chimney Rock. She turned and looked at Rachel. "Just look at me. I'm so burned, my skin is peeling off."

Rachel smiled. "Yes, but your skin will heal and you'll be just as beautiful as you were before."

Katie looked at Rachel's golden toned skin and for the first time in her life wished she was dark. It didn't seem fair that she burned while everyone else got a little darker.

She gave a very unladylike snort. "What I will be is freckled and splotchy from burning. Besides, my face hurts and so does the back of my neck. Tommy is fair, too, but he isn't burning like this. I'm thirsty, too."

Rachel sighed. "I know. I miss Ash Hollow already." She laughed. "All but the Indians."

Katie looked about the barren, sandy countryside. Scraggly-looking brush seemed to be the only vegetation and odd-looking rock formations rose out of the sand. Jason had told her after reading from his guide that Chimney Rock was the beginning of several landmarks they would see.

Susanna ran ahead of them, obviously anxious for the outing.

"Hey, wait and I'll walk with you." The girls turned at Tommy's voice.

"I thought you went to see Amanda. What happened?" Katie asked.

Tommy shrugged. "She said she didn't feel well."

Concern shone from Rachel's eyes. "Nothing serious, I hope?"

Tommy turned his smile on her. "No, I don't think so. Now, how about I escort you three ladies to see the famous Chimney Rock?"

Katie glanced at Rachel who smiled at Tommy. "That would be fine, wouldn't it, Katie?"

Before she could answer, they heard Jason's voice calling. "Hey! Wait a minute."

They stopped until he caught up. "Mind if I tag along?"

Tommy grinned. "Might as well. That's what I'm doing."

Susanna ran back to them and reached for Jason with her head tilted. Will you carry me, Jason?"

"Suzy!" Katie felt her face grow even hotter than the burn on it. "You can't be asking people things like that."

"That's all right." Jason squatted in front of Susanna. "Hop on my back and I'll give you a piggy-back ride."

Susanna giggled as she obeyed. "I'm riding a piggy's back."

"Susanna Donovan!" This time Katie felt the flush all the way to her toes.

Tommy and Jason laughed. Rachel touched Katie's arm. "It's all right, Katie. I don't think Jason minds. Actually, it looks like he's having as much fun as Suzy is."

Katie watched Jason run ahead with the little girl bouncing on his back and she had to agree with Rachel. He didn't seem to mind. He obviously cared for her little sister. Admiration for a man who would play with a child when he didn't have to crept into Katie's heart.

The rock was a large outcropping of sandstone that sloped gently upward to an eroded spiral that looked very much like a finger pointing at the sky. Others milled around the wide base of the rock commenting on interesting things about it. A man pointed toward the top of the formation. "I read in the guide book that the top of the spiral reaches 350 feet above the ground we're standing on right now."

Katie turned to Jason with a teasing smile. "Now why didn't you tell us that?"

He grinned. "Hadn't got to it yet."

Tommy grabbed Rachel's hand and tugged. "Come on.

74

Let's see what it looks like from the other side."

Rachel laughed and ran with him as they hurried away. Katie stared at them before she realized she needed to close her mouth. Maybe Tommy liked Rachel after all. When they disappeared from view, she turned back toward Jason and Suzy as they inspected the rock. Suzy looked down at Katie from her superior height on Jason's shoulders and a frown crossed her face.

"I'm sorry, Katie, but I guess you're too big for Jason to pick up, so you can't see as good as me."

Katie stared at the rock while her face burned.

Still, she heard the laughter in Jason's voice. "Oh, I don't know. Katie's not so big. I think I might be able to manage."

Katie whirled away and sat on a nearby rock with her back to them. This was the absolutely last time she would take Susanna anywhere near other people. Never had she been so embarrassed. Jason's amused chuckle did nothing to help her mood. Tommy and Rachel's voices, chatting like old friends, drifted to her. She stood and called to them. "We need to get back."

"Aw, Katie, do we have to?" Susanna's mouth drew down in a pout.

Katie refused to give in. "Yes, I don't want to leave Mama with all the work."

She was glad when the others seemed ready to go. But as soon as she reached their wagon and saw her mother's face, she knew something was wrong. "Mama, what is it? Are you all right?"

Mama shook her head. "I'm fine, Katie. A baby died today. He was stillborn. His parents are taking it awfully hard."

An innocent baby. Why did that have to happen? Katie's head spun as her heart ached for the parents who'd lost a child. "Who was it, Mama?"

"Their name is Parker. Just a young couple. This was their first child." She leaned against the wagon as if her strength gave out.

"Is the mother. . . ?" Katie's heart pounded. If the mother died, too . . .

"No, she's fine. It's just one of those things, Katie." Mama straightened and smiled. "I'm sure they'll have more children later. It's just hard for them right now."

But that wasn't all that was bothering Mama. Katie stood still while her mother turned away. Was there a problem with Mama's baby? Did she fear she'd lose him as she'd lost Karl? She very well might. Katie folded her arms across her chest and looked up at the sky. *Why? What is the reason for suffering? The innocent shouldn't die. They shouldn't be burned like poor little Mary Beth. Why must this happen?*

When no answer came she closed her eyes and lowered her face. This horrible trail had no respect for the children regardless of their innocence. First Karl and Mary Beth. Now a baby boy died for no reason. He hadn't even had a chance to live. Why did God allow it? How many more would die before they reached Oregon?

~*~

Jason laughed out load.

"Mind sharing the joke?" Ma Taylor sat beside him on the wagon seat. Pa was walking. Said he needed to stretch his legs. More likely he wanted to lighten the load.

Jason grinned. "No joke. I just thought of something funny."

"Tell me what it is. I need a laugh." Ma waited with a half-smile on her face.

Oh sure, tell about how Katie got so embarrassed by her little sister's comments? Ma would be sure to make something out of him remembering the look on her face after so many days had passed. He shook his head.

"Hmm. Did something happen I don't know about?" She kept her attention on him.

He chuckled. "It isn't anything really funny. Remember, I've told you about the Donovans."

"The ones who lost their young son before we left Kansas?" Her voice softened.

He nodded. "Yeah, Karl's family. His little sister is a real cute kid. I gave her a piggy-back ride out to Chimney Rock when we were stopped back there."

"This must be funny. That was a while back." She waited as if there were more.

He shrugged. "That's it."

"What do you mean, that's it?" She huffed. "I'm waiting to hear what Suzy's older sister did."

Jason swung to stare at her. "I take it you know the family better than I thought."

Ma laughed. "Do you think I sit right here in camp while you're out gallivanting around making friends. I've made my share of friends, too. This may be a large company, but we're usually pretty close to the Donovan wagon as if you haven't noticed."

His heart took a nosedive before it began pounding just as it had when she'd caught him in a forbidden act when he was a kid. Only this time he hadn't done anything wrong. Certainly not forbidden. Well, sort of discouraged maybe. Okay, strongly cautioned against. Becoming romantically attracted to Katie Donovan wasn't the best thing he could do. How many times had Ma and Pa both cautioned him to find a girl who believed and shared his commitment to the Lord? No matter how he tried to twist the truth, Katie had all but told him she didn't believe.

But maybe he'd read the situation wrong. She'd gone through a hard time and still hurt from the loss of her brother. With time and patience, she'd come through and grow even stronger in her faith. At least, that's what he hoped.

"It's Katie Donovan, isn't it?" Ma's soft voice penetrated his thoughts.

He blinked and slanted a look toward her. "How do you do that? I didn't want you to know how I feel about her. I don't know if she's serving the Lord. I've been holding off, waiting to find out first."

"That's wise." Ma patted his hand. "I've been praying with her mother for the salvation of the entire family. That poor woman. Her husband doesn't believe, and neither do her children. She carries a heavy load."

Jason swallowed his disappointment. So Katie wasn't just a hurting believer. "I'll add my prayers to yours."

"I'm glad, but please be careful. Be friends with Katie and

Tommy, but don't lose your heart yet."

He nodded. He couldn't lose his heart now because he'd already done that.

~*~

"Here, can you put this back for me?" Mama handed a cast-iron skillet to Katie. "I don't think I'll use it after all."

Katie took the skillet and turned to hang it on the side of the wagon out of the way when she saw the tall, lean figure of Jason Barnett coming toward them. An unexpected racing of her pulse surprised her. She briefly closed her eyes and shook her head, denying the stirrings of her heart that she couldn't believe and wouldn't accept. Jason was Tommy's friend. He meant nothing to her.

His face broke into a smile when she looked back. He lifted the wide-brimmed felt hat that usually sat at an angle on his head. "Hi. You in the mood for a walk?"

She couldn't stop the smile that pulled at her mouth. "Sure, I'll see if Tommy wants to go, too."

"Don't think so." He shook his head. "I just saw him heading toward Scott's Bluff."

The train was camped just past the famous bluffs. Katie figured she'd help Mama sort and repack the wagon during their half-day rest before they reached Fort Laramie. If they restocked there, they'd need room for their purchases. "I don't know if I should go. How about Rachel? I'm sure she would like to."

Jason chuckled. "She's already gone—with Tommy."

"With Tommy? They were together?" Katie stared at him.

Jason nodded. "Yeah, but I don't think I saw Suzy heading out with anyone."

Katie smiled. That was the reason he asked her to go. He wanted to play horsey for Susanna again. She shook her head. "Suzy wasn't feeling well so Mama put her to bed as soon as we stopped. Do you still want me to go?"

"Sure I do. That's why I asked."

"All right. If you'll wait just a minute, I'll ask Mama if she needs my help with anything."

When she turned the corner of the wagon, Mama waved

her away. "You go ahead and have fun. It'll be at least two hours before the beans are ready and I think I'll rest with Suzy." She brushed a wayward strand of hair from her face and sighed. "I'll be glad to get to the fort where we can get some more food. I don't know how long the little we have will last."

"I know, Mama. But we should be there in a few days." Katie gave her a quick hug. "Thanks for letting me go."

Katie couldn't remember feeling so aware of a man before as she was Jason. Walking beside him without Tommy or Rachel seemed strange, but she soon forgot her awkwardness as Jason talked about his early years.

"My parents died when I was young. I don't really remember either of them."

"How terrible. Who raised you?"

"My grandparents, but we lost Grandpa when a cow stepped on him. Not right off." Jason looked toward the bluff. "He lived several weeks after that. Grandma and I stayed on the farm and tried to keep it going, but I was still so young. I couldn't do the job of a man, and she couldn't either. I was fifteen when she died."

Katie searched his face and saw a hint of pain even as he smiled. "I had a run-down farm and a few animals so I hired out to Grandma's neighbors. They offered to buy the place and take me on, too. I liked them, and they seemed to like me all right, so we made the deal."

"The Taylors?" She guessed.

"Right." He grinned. "They are the closest to parents I've ever had. They saw that I finished school and taught me just about everything I know." He grew serious then. "I guess the most important thing they taught me was about the love of God."

"Then, you're more than just their hired hand." Katie spoke her thought aloud.

Jason grinned. "They've always made me feel as if I'm their son. To me, they're Ma and Pa."

When they arrived at the high bluff, Katie looked around, recognizing several people from the train, but didn't see her brother. "I wonder where Tommy and Rachel are?"

"Maybe they're in another part. Are you too tired to walk around a little?"

"Of course not." She took a step landing on loose rock.

"Be careful." Jason's hand closed around Katie's arm to steady her. His touch seemed to burn through her flesh, and she was aware of his nearness in a way she had not expected and wasn't sure she liked. She took a deep breath and let it out. What on earth was wrong with her? Her confused feelings angered her and she jerked her arm away.

"I'm fine. I wasn't going to fall, and even if I did I suppose I could get back up without help."

The hurt in his sky blue eyes reprimanded her so she softened her voice. "I appreciate your help. I guess I just wasn't expecting it."

She crossed to a large flat rock and sat down. When he sat beside her, she turned to look up the sloping base of the bluff to the wall of rock that rose straight above them for several hundred feet. He didn't speak. She'd probably hurt his feelings. And no wonder. What got into her sometimes to be so rude? She searched her mind for something to say. "Everything is brown. I'd love to see some green again."

His voice sounded soft so close beside her. "I know. Except for the green of your eyes, I doubt there's any within miles of here."

Katie looked quickly at him then away. She twisted her fingers in her lap. She shouldn't have left camp alone with him. Not that she feared him. More likely she feared her reaction to his nearness.

"That must have been a terrible ordeal for Hiram Scott."

"Who?" Katie looked up, puzzled.

Jason grinned. "Hiram Scott was a fur trader who got sick while on an expedition in 1829. His companions went off and left him rather than risk their own lives. He crawled sixty miles across the dry, barren plain to this bluff. After that torturous crawl, his strength gave out and he simply lay down and died."

Compassion filled Katie's heart. "How terrible. How did you know about it?"

"I read it in the guide just before we came."

"Oh, you! I should've known the way you sounded like you were quoting something." Katie laughed, and his laughter blended with hers.

While others milled around them, Katie began to relax as she and Jason sat on the rock and talked. As the shadows crept across them, the air became cooler. Katie jumped up. "Oh, no, my mother will be sick with worry. She said to come back in a couple of hours, and I'll bet we've been gone twice that long."

Jason took her hand as they walked toward camp, and she didn't resist. Instead, she nestled her hand in his and felt the rightness of doing so. Although, when Tommy met them not far out of camp, she pulled her hand away and Jason didn't stop her.

"Where have you two been?" Tommy's expression held a mixture of disbelief and suspicion as he looked from one to the other.

"The same place you and Rachel were, if my source is right." Katie retorted.

Tommy had the grace to look guilty. "Yeah, I guess I don't have much room to talk. I wanted to go to the bluff so when Rachel happened along, I asked her if she'd like to go with me. Actually, we just got back a few minutes ago. Mama was a little worried so I told her I'd see if I could find you."

"We didn't see you out at the bluff." Katie said.

"I assure you, we were there. After the walk out there, we sat down to rest and ended up talking for longer than we realized." He grinned. "Did you know that every hair on my head has been counted?"

"By Rachel?" Katie thought the idea was preposterous, but a scene with Rachel going through Tommy's hair one by one came to her mind.

Tommy laughed. "Rachel told me that. She didn't count them."

Jason grinned at Katie. "I think she's referring to the Scripture in Matthew that says God knows even the very number of hairs on our heads."

"Oh, well that makes more sense." Katie picked up her pace. The sooner she got away from both of them, the better she'd like it. Maybe Clay would come over tonight so she could enjoy herself.

But Clay didn't come. Katie went to bed early and fell asleep almost instantly. Her dreams were devoid of Clay. Instead they were filled with a tall, lean figure wearing Kentucky jeans, a blue cotton shirt, covered by a buckskin vest and a wide-brimmed felt hat set at a jaunty angle atop a head of golden-blond hair.

Chapter 10

*K*atie fixed her sights on Laramie Peak and concentrated on putting one foot in front of the other. The few days to Fort Laramie had stretched to more than a week and she was tired of the constant walking. She hated the sand and heat. And they were running out of food.

She turned to Rachel. "We'll be at the fort as soon as we cross the river and I will be so glad."

Rachel smiled. "I know. It seems like this last week has been as long as all the rest put together. Look over there." She pointed to a small thicket of cottonwood trees growing near the edge of the Laramie River. "If that isn't a sight for sore eyes, I don't know what is."

Katie gave a short laugh. "I've longed to see something alive and growing after all this sand. There's some grass, too. On the hills over there. Isn't it beautiful?"

"Yes, and the animals will think it's delicious."

The next day they arrived at the river crossing where Katie was shocked to see Indian men helping. She ran up to her father. "What is going on?"

"Looks like we're getting some help."

"Is that safe?" Katie knew the river was broad and its banks were rough and rocky so they could probably use the help, but Indians frightened her.

"I'd reckon if it wasn't, Jeb would stop it."

When they reached the opposite bank, teepees set up outside the fort came into view. Maybe Jeb Larson didn't know what he was doing. The Indians, who had helped, ran toward the teepees where they joined their waiting squaws and children. Katie's heart sank. The wagon train would be camped for two days outside the fort next to a temporary Indian village.

Katie divided her attention between the Indians and the fort as she helped her mother prepare for the evening meal. Fort Laramie, primarily a trading post, sat near the foot of the hills. The low, oblong stone building she'd caught a glimpse of when they arrived held supplies for which the emigrants were eager to trade. Far too many in the wagon train had already started rationing food after almost two months on the trail. Maybe Dad would bring back something different than the beans, bread, and dried apples they had been eating.

As she and her mother got the fire going and beans on to boil, Katie glanced about for Jason. She hadn't seen him since their trip to Scott's Bluff. He was as unpredictable as Clay. Why did she always attract men who only showed up when they wanted to? His absence was becoming conspicuous and she could only assume he was avoiding her. Clay probably was, too.

But something had happened between her and Jason that day at the bluff. She felt it when they touched hands and saw it in his eyes as he looked at her. To believe he would avoid her now hurt more than she wanted to admit.

She sighed as she stirred beans into the boiling water. Something must be wrong with her. She was attracted to Clay, yet just the thought of Jason set her pulse to racing. Since his sister's accident, Clay barely noticed her and now Jason avoided her.

Her father striding into camp interrupted her gloomy thoughts. "Mary, I need to talk to you. Those Indians are demanding a party."

"A party?" Mama straightened from the fire where she had just poked another stick. "I don't understand."

Dad sat on an overturned barrel. "They want us to give them a party tomorrow night. They want music, but more than that, they want our food and whisky."

"Oh, dear." Mama sat down in her rocking chair. "I suppose they feel they have it coming after helping us cross the river."

"You'd better believe that's what they think." Dad spat to the side. "We'll have to feed that mob of savages over there with what little we have to last us the next three or four months and most of us don't even have enough to keep ourselves going that long."

"Did you get anything at the trading post?" Mama looked hopefully at the bundles he had dropped near his feet.

He nodded. "A little. The pickings were slim, but it would have been enough without this party."

"Is there any way we can get out of it?"

Dad shook his head. "No, if we don't have a party, they'll never let us go through their territory and come out alive."

The next day as clouds gathered in the southwest, the tantalizing aroma of dried apple pie, fresh bread, and cake drifted through the air. Katie glanced over at the Indian village where several Indians sat on the ground just outside their teepees.

"Look at them." She complained to her mother. "They're lazing around over there watching us. They remind me of vultures waiting for the kill."

Mama shook her head with a sad smile. "Pay them no mind. We'll be leaving tomorrow. I suppose the loss of some of our supplies won't stop us. Besides, a party might be a good thing. We will show them that white men can be friends and pay their debts. After all, they did help us cross the river."

"Mama, it was all of three feet deep! I really think we could have crossed without them."

Mama smiled. "I know, Katie. I know." She glanced up at the overcast sky. "Maybe it will rain so we won't have to stay long."

Katie shrugged. "Maybe. I guess we can hope for rain. Suzy felt hot to me while ago. She's lying down now."

"I know. Seems she goes from one sickness to another. Thank the Lord nothing has been serious. I'll keep her here at the wagon tonight."

"Mama, can I stay with her?" Katie frowned. There would be drinking tonight with the Indians, and Dad didn't need to be near whiskey. He'd done so well avoiding it since they left Missouri. But without Mama's presence, he might slide back into his old ways.

Her mother gave her a sharp look. "There's bound to be

dancing and your friends will all be there."

"That's all right. I'd rather stay with Suzy. We'll be fine here. At least we'll be away from those Indians." Katie shuddered.

Mama looked across at the Indian village and frowned. "All right. Maybe it would be for the best."

That evening Katie arranged a mattress and some pillows at the back of the wagon where she and Susanna could watch the activities. A makeshift table in the center of the wagon circle held a feast that the people of the train would sorely miss when they returned to the trail. The fiddle started its call to the dancers, and Katie's toes wanted to tap. How she would love to join the couples moving together to begin the dance. The other instruments joined in and lively music soon filled the night. Hands clapped and feet stomped to keep time. Several people moved forward to dance, but Clay didn't join them. Katie saw him standing on the sidelines watching for several minutes before he turned and walked away and she lost sight of him.

"I can't see good." Susanna squirmed, trying to get closer to the opening in the wagon.

Katie pulled her onto her lap. "Is that better?"

At Susanna's nod, she looked out, letting her hand brush her little sister's hair back from her warm face.

The Indians drew her attention with frightening fascination. Their copper-tinted skin shone in the light from the campfires as they greedily devoured the food. She hated the sight of them, and she shouldn't. Really, she had no right to fear or dislike them. Not personally, since they'd never done anything to her other than at Ash Hollow. And those were only boys having fun. Mama always said people usually confused fear for prejudice. That had to be her problem because she certainly feared Indians. She mentally shrugged and turned her attention toward her fellow travelers to see if she could recognize anyone in the large crowd.

Her parents stood talking to Mr. and Mrs. Taylor. The Taylors seemed to be very nice people. No wonder Jason cared so much for them.

She turned her attention elsewhere. Lately, Jason seemed to

have taken over her thoughts and dreams. He was a good friend and she liked him. But their interests and beliefs were too different for anything more. She needed to remember that.

"Do you see anyone you know, Suzy?" Katie pointed toward a group of young ladies. "Look, there's Tommy's friend, Amanda."

"Uh huh." Susanna didn't act interested. She seemed content to lie still and listen to the music.

Tommy didn't appear to be anywhere in sight. After their trip to Chimney Rock, he'd been spending more and more time with Rachel while Amanda had been keeping company with a young man named Jonathan Thomas. Rachel would make Tommy a wonderful wife. Not that Tommy or Rachel acted like that would happen. When Katie even hinted such a thing to either of them, they laughed at her.

Katie searched the crowd and didn't find Rachel either. Maybe she was with Tommy someplace. A distant roll of thunder brought her attention to the dark sky.

"Hiding from our guests, are you?" Jason appeared at the end of the wagon.

Katie jumped, and her heart thudded. "You could give a person some warning, you know."

"Sorry, I assumed you saw me coming." He grinned. "You were too busy watching those Indians, weren't you?"

When she didn't answer, he said, "I don't think they'll attack tonight. Not as long as they can stuff their stomachs. Besides, I imagine the rain will send them and us running for cover before this party is over."

"Suzy is sick." Katie patted her little sister's shoulder.

"Oh, I didn't even see you, Suzy." Jason reached out and touched her check. "I'm sorry you're not feeling well. I don't think you'd like this party, anyway."

Susanna didn't move from Katie's lap, but she smiled at her friend. "Why not, Jason?"

He pointed toward the far side of the gathering where a small group of men, both white and Indian, were clustered together. They passed a jug of whiskey from one to the other, laughing and talking in loud voices Katie couldn't understand with the music and other voices drowning them out.

Katie glanced at her father. He stood with his arm around Mama as they visited with another couple. To her knowledge, he had not taken a drink since the night he lost their home. If no other good came of his folly that night, at least he had given up alcohol. And gambling, too.

"Those men are being noisy." Susanna stirred and leaned against the tailgate, getting closer to Jason.

"I don't think they'll get out of hand, though." Jason patted Suzy's fingers curled over the end of the wagon. "Mr. Colton is keeping a good eye on them."

"Have you seen Tommy or Rachel?" Katie asked.

Jason nodded. "A while ago. They were sitting by a campfire reading."

"Reading?"

"Yes, they had a Bible and seemed very interested in it."

Katie stared at Jason. He looked serious. Rachel must have done some hard talking to get Tommy to read a Bible with her. He put up with Mama's Bible reading out of respect for their mother. Still, if Tommy had become attracted to Rachel, he might suffer through another Bible reading just to be with her.

A distant rumble shook the sky and Jason straightened.

Katie turned to see what had captured his attention. A couple of men were apparently in the middle of an argument. Her heart dipped. Why did grown men become so stupid when they drank whiskey?

One held his fist up before the other. Their faces were twisted with anger, and they appeared to be hurling insults at each other.

"I think I'll walk over that way and see if Mr. Colton needs any help."

As Jason started away, Katie called to him. "Please be careful, Jason."

He flashed a wide grin her way before striding toward the ruckus that was becoming increasingly louder. How like Jason to step in and try to help! Katie watched him, admiring the way he walked without hesitation into a situation where he could get hurt just because it was the right thing to do.

A streak of lightening flashed across the sky, followed by another touching the far southern horizon. Scattered rain drops fell. Indians and whites both moved toward shelter. Katie watched Jason until he stood with a few other men in a semi-circle around the two fighting men. Katie recognized her father beside Jason.

"Looks like a storm is brewing." Katie startled at her mother's voice. She turned to watch her climb into the front of the wagon and began securing the canvas covering against the promised storm.

"Mama, a couple of men are fighting." She turned back to see one of the men take a swing and miss the other.

"I'm sure it won't last long. There's nothing like a good drenching rain to bring a man to his senses. Look how the wind's picking up. Help me get these end flaps down before we get soaked. We need to make some more room for Dad and Tommy, too."

Great drops of rain splattered against the canvas as Katie moved to help her mother. A strong puff of wind caught the canvas and jerked it from her hands. She grabbed it as a jagged streak of lightening cut across the sky, followed immediately by a loud clap of thunder.

Mr. Colton's voice rang out. "You men go on and take care of your wagons. We're about to be caught in a downpour."

When the two men didn't respond, Mr. Colton and Jason grabbed one by the arms while Jeb Larson and Katie's father grabbed the other. Within seconds a drenching rain fell on them, and just as Mama had said, the fight ended as quickly as it started.

Katie caught the canvas and held tight as she secured it. Tommy stuck his head in and grinned. "You all need some help?"

Their father climbed in behind him. They finished securing the wagon for the night. Katie wondered at Tommy's cheerful attitude. She wanted to ask about his time spent with Rachel, but didn't dare with the entire family so close. She promised herself that the first chance she got in the morning, she would find out what was going on between her brother and her friend.

Chapter 11

*T*he driving rain lasted until early the next morning and dampened more than the men who had been so intent on a fight the night before. Soaked bedding would have to be aired as soon as possible to keep it from molding.

Mr. Colton delayed their departure one more half day to allow for drying. Katie pulled the three mattresses out and leaned them against the wagon. "Thank goodness they're only wet on the edge." She ran her hand over the last one as she had the other two. They wouldn't take long to dry.

"That was some party we had last night, wasn't it?" Tommy walked up behind her.

She swung to meet him with a frown. "One we could have done without."

Tommy's blue eyes twinkled above his smile. "Maybe, but it's one night I'll never forget."

Katie stared at her brother. "Did something happen between you and Rachel last night?"

"Rachel?" A puzzled frown crossed Tommy's handsome face.

"Yes, Rachel." Katie tried to keep from raising her voice. Surely, he knew what she meant. "You were with her last night, weren't you?"

"Yeah." He looked at Katie. "You think that—" A smile stretched his lips until he broke out in a laugh. "Always the romantic, aren't you?"

Before she could think of a good retort, a serious expression crossed his face. "What happened, little sister, was I became a new man last night. Your friend has been talking to me, explaining things to me. Ever since we were at Chimney Rock. All those things Mama's been saying all these years finally came together for me. Rachel prayed with me and now I have peace inside like I never dreamed was possible. Maybe you should think about doing the same."

He started away and stopped. "Oh, Jeb wants me to go back out on a scouting trip. You can take care of the cows, can't you?"

Katie nodded and stared after her brother as he walked away whistling Amazing Grace.

Tommy didn't like church music.

~*~

Katie slumped in the saddle. She was hot. She was tired. And she was thirsty. After the party at Fort Laramie, they'd been forced to ration their food so she was also hungry. They were in buffalo country, but all she ever saw of a buffalo were chips scattered here and there in the sand. She amused herself by thinking of a huge buffalo steak with some of her mother's fluffy mashed potatoes and gravy. Her stomach growled.

It grumbled again, only this time she didn't feel it. The rumble continued and she realized it wasn't her stomach, but something in the air. It sounded more like distant thunder. Except, this thunder kept coming and the sky was as clear and blue as any she'd ever seen.

Star's nostrils flared, and she whinnied in fear. The cattle, too, acted nervous. Something was terribly wrong, but Katie had no idea what it was. Fear moved through her body sapping her strength so that she clung to the saddle.

The ominous rumble grew louder by the minute. Katie's heart pounded. At a sudden shout behind her, she jerked around. Clay rode his horse furiously toward the wagons. He came toward her shouting something she couldn't understand. She only recognized the fear it brought. As he galloped past, she finally heard.

"Buffalo! Stampeding this way!"

Tommy followed him. He reined Midnight in, causing the big black horse to lift its front legs and prance to the side. Tommy yelled above the bawling cattle and the growing thunder of a thousand buffalo. He pointed to the side. "Get the cattle out of the way."

Jeb raced past. "Get those wagons moving."

Mr. Colton rode alongside the wagons urging the drivers to pick up the pace. He encouraged them. "We can outrun the stampede."

For precious moments, Katie froze while she took in the sudden burst of activity. What would happen if they couldn't get out of the way?

Drivers all along the lines grabbed their whips and lashed at the oxen, yelling in excitement.

"Katie, I can't help you." Tommy rode into her line of vision, and she focused on him. "Can you do it?"

Mr. Colton rode past shouting. "Move your cattle to the south side of the wagons." He repeated every few feet so all those working with the animals heard.

Katie kicked Star causing her to rear up, front hooves fighting the air. As she came down, Katie yelled at the top of her lungs and was relieved to see the cows take off in a run with Star close behind them.

Katie scarcely saw where she was going as hooves and wagon wheels turned the train into a huge cloud of dust. Wagons creaked in protest while the oxen ran from drivers pushing them beyond their endurance. Women and children ran with all their might after the wagons, trying to keep up.

Still, the horrible thundering of the stampede came ever closer, filling Katie's heart with fear. How could they possibly get out of the way when the buffalo were running faster than they were?

"Haw." Katie yelled and allowed Star to take the lead in forcing their cattle into position, still pushing them forward as fast as they could run.

With her cows in position, Katie glanced around to see what was going on. Tommy galloped past on Midnight toward the north side of the wagons. He pulled his rifle from its sheath as he went. She lost sight of him in the billowing cloud of dust, but moments later she heard a command ring out.

"Ready, fire!"

A volley of rifle shots filled the air and Star danced to the side. Katie quickly had her under control, but she couldn't control her rapidly beating heart. Had the men shot the buffalo? Surely, there were too many to shoot. If every bullet found its mark there would still be a thousand more of the crazed beasts coming. Loud bellows filled the air even above the bawling cattle. Surely, that was the buffalo. They must still be stampeding.

A shout went up from the men. Their voices grew in volume as their yells swept throughout the long wagon train. Happy, victorious shouts vibrated through the cloud of dust until she wanted to laugh and add her voice to theirs. Surely, the train had been saved. She was sure of it when the wagons began slowing to a stop. She slowed, too then Tommy emerged from the slowly settling dust.

He rode up beside her, a wide grin on his face. "We did it. Jeb said they would turn if we shot into them, and they did. I think I hit one."

Katie stared at him as her heart rate changed from fear to excitement. "How on earth could you tell? If a bunch of men shot into a bunch of animals, how would you know if your bullet went wild or killed one of them?"

Tommy laughed. "I have no idea, but I still think I hit one."

Katie laughed, too. It felt good to laugh after the tense and dangerous time they had just gone through.

She and Tommy drove their exhausted cattle into the center of the night ring that slowly formed well away from the still stampeding buffalo. Katie felt sorry for the oxen as they looked almost dead on their feet after the hard run. She took care of Star while Tommy cared for Midnight then they walked together to their wagon.

Mr. Colton stood in the center of a circle of men. His voice carried to Katie as she walked past. "We'll camp here today and tomorrow. The animals need a rest. I don't know if the counts in, but there's at least a dozen buffalo to butcher. Let's get busy, folks, and have us a community supper tonight. Each family should bring a dish to go with the meat."

Voices raised in agreement, and Katie's heart leapt at the thought. She looked at Tommy. "It'll be a party."

He laughed. "Yep, and you never miss a party, do you?"

"Not many." She didn't mention the Indian party at Fort Laramie that she'd chosen to miss. The Indians had devoured their food. None of them would have much to contribute tonight, but with so much meat who would care?

Rachel ran toward them. "Are you all right?"

Tommy spoke for him and Katie. "Sure. How about you?"

"I'm fine." She rubbed her arms as if she were cold. "I was really frightened for a while. I'm glad we'll have some meat now."

"Yeah, me too." Tommy grinned. "I think I shot one of the buffalo."

Rachel's eyes brightened. "Really? That's wonderful."

Katie looked from Tommy to Rachel. If they knew she was there, they sure didn't act like it. Why they refused to admit the attraction they shared for each other was a mystery. She shook her head. "I'm going to check on Mama."

As Katie stepped toward the wagon, her mother stepped down the ramp from the back and opened the box on the side. She lifted out a frying pan.

Tommy nodded toward her. "There she is. She seems all right."

Katie sighed. "She probably is, but I wish she'd rest once in a while. She never stops working."

"I'd better go help my mother, too," Rachel said. "I'll see you later at supper."

As Katie worked beside her mother, she could still hear the thundering of the stampeding buffalo. Two hours later, the last buffalo disappeared over the far horizon. So many large and dangerous animals could have done damage to the train. Lives could have been lost if not for the quick actions of everyone working together.

That evening, Katie sat to eat with Rachel and Tommy on a quilt spread on the ground. When she saw Jason heading toward them, her heart raced. He stopped at the edge of the quilt and smiled. "Got room for one more?"

Tommy moved closer to Rachel, leaving a spot beside Katie. Jason grinned at her and sat down just as Mr. Colton asked everyone to stand.

"Let's bow our heads in prayers." After a moment, he began. "Father God, we thank You for protection today and for the meat You have provided. Bless it and those of us gathered here tonight in Your name we pray."

Two lines formed, one on either side of several makeshift tables that had been put together with odds and ends of furniture and boards.

With her plate fuller than she remembered seeing it in several days, Katie sat again on the quilt between Jason and Rachel and ate her supper. They talked about the stampede and other things on the trail until Tommy gave a laugh.

"Rachel is giving me mean looks so I'd better say something before I'm in all kinds of trouble."

Katie looked at Rachel. A flush stained her lightly tanned cheeks. So something had been going on between those two, and Tommy waited until now to tell. Katie leaned forward with an expectant smile. Tommy couldn't find anyone better than Rachel.

"Last night something special happened to me." Tommy looked at Jason and his eyes sparkled. "I've already told Katie."

Katie sent a frown toward her brother. He hadn't told her about him and Rachel.

Jason grinned. "Let me guess. You found Someone special who was not lost, but who has been looking for you all your life because you were lost."

Tommy's laughter rang out, and Rachel smiled. Tommy said, "I never heard it put that way before, but yes, that's exactly what happened. I'm glad you understand."

Katie looked at the other three. Had they lost their minds? She didn't understand a word they said. Then she remembered her brother's words.

All those things Mama's been saying all these years finally came together for me last night. Rachel prayed for me.

Katie's heart sank. Tommy had come to Christ just as Mama said everyone must do. Nothing had happened between Rachel and Tommy after all. Katie looked at Rachel's glowing expression. The poor girl. Rachel loved Tommy. How could she look so happy when he didn't return her love?

Then from across the crowd of people, quick, toe-tapping music lifted above every other sound and tired as they were, couples moved into a cleared area to dance. Katie watched them, knowing that she would not be dancing that night. Rachel and Jason didn't believe in it. Tommy probably didn't either now. At least Mama would be happy.

She was tired, anyway. She sat on the quilt, listening to the music and to the others talk. Rachel turned and looked out at the gathering. "So many people just in our company. Ours is only one of many wagon trains that go west each year. I wonder why so many face the dangers and hardships to make this trip."

Jason shrugged. "Many reasons. Probably as many as there are families here tonight. Why don't we each tell our story and see what we can learn?"

Katie's heart sank. She wasn't proud of the events that led to their father's decision to join the train and didn't know if she wanted to share them.

Rachel said, "Why don't you go first, Jason? Tell us why the Taylors would leave their farm and start over so far from home. And you, too. Why did you come with them?"

Jason smiled. "There's not much story to tell. We'd had a couple of bad years weather wise on the farm. Mr. Taylor had been hearing of this wonderful land in the northwest and wanted to go. I guess I have a bit of an adventurous nature because I liked the idea of starting over in a new place where I could have land of my own. I love the Taylors as if they were my own parents, but I do want my own land. This may not be an easy way to get it, but once we're there, it'll be free."

Tommy nodded. "I imagine most people here would have a similar tale to tell. The pull of the free fertile land in the Oregon Territory is strong." He looked at Rachel. "You're next."

Rachel smiled as sadness crept into her large brown eyes. "Uncle Joseph was without doubt the greatest man I've ever known. He was also a slave on the plantation where we lived."

Katie forgot the dance as she listened to Rachel's story.

"Another slave got sick one day, and Uncle Joseph tried to help him by doing his work. The owner became very angry and ordered my pa to whip both of them. When Pa refused, he got some other men to help. They tied Pa to the fence where he could see, but couldn't stop them, and they beat the other slave to death."

Rachel choked and wiped tears from her eyes before she went on. "Uncle Joseph passed out so they stopped. They let my pa go and told him we had to be gone from the plantation by sundown the next day. They also told him he had to bury the two slaves. To make a long story short, Uncle Joseph didn't die that night. We couldn't leave him there alive, so we put him in our extra wagon in a swinging bed that Pa fixed for him so he wouldn't be bumped around as we traveled."

"How did you get permission to do that?" Tommy asked.

Rachel smiled. "We didn't. Pa and Daniel put sand in the pine box meant for Uncle Joseph and went ahead with the funeral. I saw the owner and his son watching from the ridge, but they didn't look inside the boxes. They think Uncle Joseph is buried in the slaves' cemetery."

"So, you had no place to go and decided to start over in Oregon?" Jason asked.

Rachel nodded. "That's right. Oregon is free country without slavery." She looked down at her hands in her lap. "But Uncle Joseph didn't make it. He died before we reached Missouri. Of course, he wasn't really my uncle, but I respected him and miss him." Rachel turned to Tommy. "Now it's your turn."

Tommy lifted his eyebrows. "I wish I could say we left for honorable reasons, but I'd be lying if I did."

Katie looked down as her brother went on.

"Dad's always had a liking for the whiskey bottle. About once a week, he'd visit the local saloon where he could drink and play cards, too. The last time he went, he had what he called a bad run of luck. He lost his hand of cards and our farm."

"Oh, no." Rachel covered her mouth, her eyes wide.

"Yeah." Tommy grinned at her. "Dad's Irish and has the temper that goes with it. He couldn't face Mama if he didn't at least try to get the farm back, so he tried to reason with the man who won it. When talking didn't work, he used his fists and knocked the man's head against an iron railing. He thought he'd killed him for sure. Oregon sounded pretty good then."

"Did he?" Jason asked. "Kill the man, I mean."

Tommy shook his head. "No. The sheriff caught up with us before we got very far and told Dad he was in the clear. Considering we still had no home to go back to, he decided to turn over a new leaf and go on to Oregon. So here we are."

"He seems like a nice man." Rachel stared into Tommy's face.

Tommy nodded. "He is normally. I'll admit I'm a little surprised he's stayed sober all this time. I guess he meant it when he said he wouldn't touch the stuff again."

While Tommy told of their father's run in with the law, Katie thought of Rachel's story. Admiration for the Morgans contrasted with her feelings of resentment toward her own father. She wondered if she would ever find it in her heart to forgive him. The loss of their farm now seemed insignificant compared to the greater loss of her young brother. For that, there could be no forgiveness.

Chapter 12

*I*ndependence Rock loomed in the west. Far beyond it, at the western horizon, Devil's Gate waited. For the last two days Katie had watched the huge rock grow larger as they advanced.

Tommy rode in her direction. She pulled Star up and waited until he came alongside.

"Well, what's ahead of us?"

Tommy grinned. "Not much except that big rock you can see from here. We'll be there by nightfall."

"That big rock is famous, you know."

Tommy nodded. "I plan to take Rachel there to see it. We'll be staying over a while to take advantage of Sweetwater River. The animals need the grass, and we need the rest."

Katie brightened at his news. "Then you do like Rachel."

"I never said I didn't." Tommy laughed. "Why do you keep pushing her off on me? I like Rachel because she explains the Bible better than any preacher I've ever heard."

He turned Midnight toward the wagons. "There's more to life than love and marriage, little sister. It's time you thought of your spiritual condition instead of romance all the time."

Katie watched him ride away. He was falling for Rachel, she was sure of it. Rachel was already half in love with him. She smiled. She was young. There'd be time enough to think of religion. Right now Tommy and Rachel's blooming romance promised to be more interesting. Her smile faded as she thought of her own desert of love. Clay and Jason were both special in their own way. She might be able to fall for either of them, but Clay seemed to have lost interest in her, and Jason only wanted to be friends with Tommy and her because of the way he'd felt about Karl. She spent the rest of the day bemoaning her lack of beaus and Tommy's lack of interest in anything romantic.

The company arrived at the foot of Independence Rock and began making camp beside Sweetwater River where they found plenty of clear, sweet water and tender, green grass for the animals.

A bend in the river provided a private place for the girls and women to bathe. Katie and Rachel went early the next morning with a few other girls. Katie took a soothing bath and washed her long, auburn hair until the sunshine sparkled off the ends like spun gold.

"Oh, it feels good to be clean again." She tossed her hair back over her shoulder and dressed. She rolled down her long sleeves then lifted her wet, heavy hair from her back and combed her fingers through the strands. The sun was already out, warming the land and would be uncomfortable before long.

"I know." Rachel squeezed water from her dark brown hair. She stopped and looked at Katie. "Are you aware it's almost the fourth of July?"

Katie grinned and nodded. "That's where Independence Rock got its name. Or so I've been told. Almost all the wagon trains coming through here arrive about this same time. Independence Day equals Independence Rock."

Rachel laughed. "And where did you get all that information? From a young man we all know by the name of Jason Barnett, maybe?"

"How did you guess?" Katie climbed from the water. "He's always finding something in that guide book of his to share with us."

"Are you going to the rock?" Rachel followed. "Why don't we go together?"

Katie lifted her eyebrows. "Aren't you going with Tommy?"

A flush touched Rachel's cheeks. She shook her head. "Not that I know of."

Katie shook her head. "He told me yesterday he planned to take you and he hasn't even asked you yet?"

The color in Rachel's cheeks grew darker. "I didn't know."

"But you will go with him?"

Rachel nodded. "If he asks me. You don't mind, do you?"

Katie hurried to dress. "No, I don't mind. Actually, I mind that he didn't ask you last night. He can't expect you to drop everything and run off with him just because he wants to talk about the Bible."

Instant regret for her thoughtless words filled Katie's heart when she saw the crushed look on Rachel's face. "He told me you explain the Bible better than any preacher, but Rachel, he also told me he likes you."

A weak smile was all she got. She'd love to choke her brother. Couldn't he see what he had in Rachel? She was beautiful and smart and she was the Christian girl he wanted. Whether he knew it or not.

"Come on." Katie turned toward camp. "If Tommy doesn't show up, we'll go without him. We've got a ton of things to do before we go traipsing off to look at a big rock."

Katie found her mother struggling to take a load of laundry to the river to be washed. Katie took the bundle from her. "Mama, you shouldn't be carrying this. It's much too heavy."

Mama smiled. "I don't think it would have hurt me, Katie, but I appreciate your concern."

The clothing wouldn't be clean enough to suit her when they finished, but she kept quiet. There was no point in complaining. The river was the best place to do their wash for now. She hurried through the chores, washing and laying out the clothes to dry. She carried the basket back to camp and started to climb into the wagon to straighten it.

Her mother's hand on her arm stopped her. "Katie, if this doesn't get done today, it can wait."

"I'm sorry, Mama, I was hoping to see Independence Rock today. Tommy said he was going to take Rachel. I thought if I hurried, I could go with them."

"I see." Mama placed her hands against the small of her back to stretch. "Just the three of you?"

"I'm sure other people will go, too, but I suppose just the three of us will go together. Why?"

Mama looked especially interested in the clean clothing she was folding. "I thought Jason might be going along, too."

"Jason?" Katie's eyes grew wide. What did her mother

have in mind? "Why Jason?"

"Isn't he your friend, too?"

"He's Tommy's friend."

Mama looked at Katie. "Oh? I thought he might be your friend as well."

Katie slumped against the end of the wagon. "What exactly are you trying to say?"

Mama put a folded towel in a box with the others. "Jason is a fine Christian boy. You could do a lot worse than him, Katie."

"Oh, Mama!" Katie felt the color rise to her face. A fine Christian boy was the last thing she wanted. Someone like Clay was more to her liking. "Are you trying to marry me off?

Mama looked at her a moment. "You are plenty old enough for marriage. Yes, I would like to see you settled with a good husband, but I think today I will allow you to run off and look at Independence Rock. You've worked hard and need a little holiday."

Katie jumped up and gave her mother a quick hug. "I love you, Mama. One day I'll make you proud of me."

Mama held Katie close. "I couldn't be any more proud of you than I am right now, sweetheart. I just want your happiness."

"I am happy, Mama. Truly, I am."

~*~

Katie checked first at the Morgan's camp. "Is Rachel here?"

Mrs. Morgan shook her head. "I'm sorry, she just left with your brother. I would think you could catch them if you hurry."

"Thank you." Katie hurried away, but she didn't see them anywhere. She left the security of the wagon circle and started toward the huge rock formation whose base covered more than twenty acres. She could see others already there and a couple about halfway between the wagons and the rock, but she didn't recognize Tommy or Rachel among them.

As she came closer, she saw someone on a ledge of the rounded granite rock near the top. She took a second look then quickened her steps until she reached the base and stood looking up at Jason.

A warm smile spread slowly over his face when he looked down at her. He motioned to her. "Come on up and I'll show you something."

Katie shook her head. "I can't climb up there."

"Then I'll help you." He climbed down a few feet and reached toward her. "Take my hand, Katie."

She hesitated before placing her hand in his. Jason backed up, digging each booted foot into small crevices in the surface of the rock. Katie clung to his hand and followed. Finally, he reached the ledge again and pulled her onto it with him.

They both sank to the hard surface and rested a moment before Jason stretched his arm out, indicating the view from their perch. "Look, Katie. Feast your eyes on the beauty God has set before us."

She saw white canvas wagon tops gleaming bright in the sunshine like puffs of cotton on a lush green carpet. The long strip of blue that was Sweetwater River sparkled and seemed to wink at them as it flowed merrily on its way. The sky served as a light blue backdrop with wisps of filmy white clouds floating past.

"Now look at this." Jason pulled her up. There on the side of the rock were carved names and dates. He read one. "The Oregon Company arrived here July 26, 1843."

"Oh, how interesting." Katie read another. "J. W. Nesmith from Maine." She turned to Jason. "People have left their names behind for others to read. Are you going to do the same?"

He looked at her, his blue eyes searching deep into hers. "Do you think we should?"

"Of course." Katie nodded. The wind loosened her hair, lifting it to fly out in wild disarray.

Jason watched her for several moments before he smiled and turned away. He took his hunting knife from its sheath and began scratching. She watched until he completed his name.

Next, he added her name until it read, "Jason and Katie—July 10, 1850."

A warm tingle spread through Katie's body. Jason had linked their names together for all time and for many people to see. Did he know what that would mean to her?

When he completed the date, Jason sat back on his heels and looked at it. Then he turned and smiled at Katie. His look ignited something within her heart, and she lowered her lashes in confusion. What was this feeling so foreign to anything she'd felt around any other man? Jason was Tommy's friend and that was all. Yet the very stirring of her heart suggested something else quite different.

She jumped back when he reached toward her. Without touching her skin, he brushed a flyaway tendril of hair from her face. His voice sounded gentle, the expression on his face sad. "We'd better be getting back."

~*~

Katie watched her mother rock Suzy to sleep in the old wooden rocker. Susanna curled in her lap sharing space with the swelling that was her unborn sibling. Katie sat on a quilt on the ground apart from the others.

Mama often read from her Bible by the light of the campfire when all the work was done for the day. Tonight Tommy took her place, sitting on a barrel near the glowing campfire. He held Mama's Bible reverently in his hands.

Dad was stationed somewhere along the outer fringes of the night ring on guard duty along with fifteen other men. Together they formed a circle around the company to warn of danger that might come from any direction.

Katie's mind drifted as she listened to her brother read. She couldn't understand the change in her older brother. Since the night of the Indians' party, he was so different. Something had happened that night when he talked to Rachel. Something she didn't understand.

"Hi, can I sit here?" Rachel whispered as she settled beside Katie. "I love to hear your brother read."

"Yes, I can imagine." Katie smiled, bringing a flush to Rachel's cheeks. "Of course, you can listen, anytime you want to."

"'Jesus saith unto him, I am the way, the truth, and the life: no man cometh unto the Father, but by me.'" Tommy's voice rang out, strong and sure.

Katie looked from her brother to her mother and then at

Rachel. Did they know something she didn't? Sometimes she felt as if she didn't belong. Jason, too, she realized, made her feel that way. It was as if they were settled and peaceful like a pool of water, while her insides roared and thrashed about as a rushing river after a rain. As if she'd confronted a fork in life's road, she realized she wanted to change things. If only she knew what and how. She looked again at Tommy and sensed there was help for her in what he read. She opened her mouth to call to him when a rifle shot rang out followed by the rapid explosion of other shots. Katie's heart leapt inside.

Tommy jumped up, laying the Bible on the barrel. As in one movement, he swung into the wagon, coming out with his rifle. He joined a group of men from other wagons who were already heading toward the commotion. Katie looked at her mother and then at Rachel. Both sat with heads bowed, no doubt praying. Katie kept silent and listened over the sound of her own heartbeat for anything that would indicate what had just happened.

When Tommy came back, his face was white and his hands trembled as he laid the gun back in the wagon.

With her voice steady, Mary asked, "What is it, son? Is it your father?"

He nodded and knelt beside her, tears running down his face. His words came out in short sentences, broken by sobs. "It was Indians. They took some horses. Dad tried to stop them. The first shot was his. He hit one. Then, an arrow hit him. The men are bringing him here. Mama, I'm sorry. I'm so sorry. He's gone." Tommy broke into sobs that shook his broad shoulders.

Rachel took Susanna and carried her to the wagon as Mama pulled Tommy close. She rocked him as gently as she would Susanna. Tears ran down her cheeks, but she didn't make a sound.

Katie felt paralyzed in disbelief. How could her strong, Irish father, who literally vibrated with life, be dead? She refused to believe it. Hurt, yes, but he wasn't dead.

Then they were there. The men, quiet and reverent, laid him on the sheet that Rachel spread on the ground. They stood with bowed heads and sorrowful faces while the wagon master made plans with Mama to have the burial first thing in the morning.

Katie's heart rebelled. She stared at the still, white face she loved and refused to believe. They said her father was gone just like Karl. All the bitterness and anger she had felt toward him for bringing them on the journey rose to the surface. New anger for leaving them alone in this horrible place blossomed and tears ran down her cheeks unnoticed.

She knelt beside him, scarcely believing what had happened. She memorized his face, frozen forever in death. "Why did you do this, Daddy?" She whispered, her voice hoarse. "You had no right to bring us here and leave us to—"

Death. The word lodged in her throat. She hated him, but she loved him. Guilt for her resentful feelings swept over her. How could she carry this heavy load of unforgiveness? How could she forgive him now? How could she ever forgive herself?

Someone knelt beside her, but she didn't look up. Strong arms went around her, drawing her close, and she leaned against a buckskin-clad chest. Jason was there and he cared, but still the hurt and anger would not go away. She turned toward him, burying her face in his shoulder, as sobs shook her body.

~*~

Tommy gave up scouting and drove the wagon while Katie rode herd on the cattle every day. The pain of missing her father and the guilt of her unresolved anger toward him was so sharp she wondered if the arrow had also pierced her heart. She hated Indians with a hatred she was sure would never go away.

They were in the mountains now. The snow-covered peaks of Wind River Range hovered in the distance. Katie shivered in the thin, cool air and longed for the heat of the plains they had left several days ago. Mr. Colton continually urged the company to hurry through the high altitude as mountain fever, a sickness that caused high fever and vomiting and too often death, swept throughout the wagons. Most families were touched by the strange fever in varying degrees.

One morning Susanna refused to get out of bed. "No, Katie, my tummy hurts."

Katie's heart sank. She wanted to scream. Not Suzy, too. She forced her voice to sound normal. "What do you mean, your tummy hurts? Are you hungry?"

Susanna clamped a hand to her mouth and shook her head. Her eyes looked wide and dark in her pale face.

Katie took a step back. "All right. You stay in bed for a while. I'll tell Mama."

Even with Mama's assurance that she and Suzy would be fine, Katie walked toward the animals with leaden feet, wishing she could stay and take care of her little sister and her mother.

The next evening, when they stopped for the night, Katie saw Rachel's brother, Daniel, running toward her. Her heart lurched as her first thought was of Suzy.

Daniel cupped his mouth and called. "Katie, Rachel said for you to go to the wagon. I'll take care of your cows."

Katie's heart constricted in fear. "Is Suzy—" Tears filled her eyes and she couldn't continue.

Sympathy clouded Daniel's blue eyes, but he shook his head. "I'm sorry, I don't know. She just said to hurry and get you. You'd better go. I'll take over here."

Katie ran with her skirts slapping against her legs, stumbling across the distance to the wagon where Mama and Tommy waited with Suzy. As she ran, waves of nausea swept through her body, and she stopped for a moment to release the fear-induced heaving of her stomach. She spit vomit from her mouth and wiped her lips, angry at her own weakness. She could not be sick. She wasn't sick. It was fear and grief upsetting her stomach. That and the helpless feeling that would not go away.

Again, she ran until she reached the wagon. She grabbed the rough wooden side and hung on until the pounding in her head subsided and her breathing no longer sent searing pains through her lungs. She heard voices inside and realized they were praying for Susanna's healing.

She was still alive! Weakness washed over Katie and she sagged against the outside of the wagon. Great sobs shook her body. With her head on her arms, she cried until she felt there were no tears left.

A gentle touch on her shoulder let her know she wasn't alone. "She's going to be all right, Katie. We prayed and the fever just now broke. Suzy's better."

Katie looked up into the smiling face of her older brother. "Oh, Tommy." She launched herself into his loving arms and tears of joy rolled down her cheeks.

After a moment, Tommy's voice, sounding gentler than she ever remembered, vibrated against her ear. "Are you all right?"

Katie nodded and stepped away, wiping at her face. Rachel and Mama climbed from the wagon with smiles lighting their faces.

Mama hugged Katie. "Suzy is sleeping now, but you can see her if you want."

Katie climbed in the wagon and bent over her sleeping sister to smooth a lock of hair from her face. "Thank you, God."

She brushed her tears away and went back outside.

~*~

That night Mama got her Bible out and read Psalm 23. "The Lord is my shepherd, I shall not want."

Jason sat on the ground between Tommy and Katie. Rachel sat beside Katie with Suzy lying across their laps. The Bartlett family slipped over from their wagon and found places to sit on the ground. The Taylors brought chairs to sit in.

Mama read the fourth verse. "Yea, though I walk through the valley of the shadow of death, I will fear no evil. Thy rod and thy staff, they comfort me."

As Katie heard David's beautiful words, something stirred deep within her heart. She longed to be cared for as the sheep in the Psalm. To place the burden of life in hands strong enough to carry anything no matter how heavy. The shepherd was God, and the sheep were His people. She wasn't His, and she couldn't expect Him to care for her as one of His own. She looked at the others—Jason, Tommy, Rachel, and Mama. If only she could replace the turmoil in her heart with the peace she saw reflected on each of their faces as they listened to God's promises. A deep longing welled in her heart. Oh, how she wanted to give up the hurt and rebellion.

Chapter 13

"*M*ama, please sit down and rest. I can do this." Katie pulled the second mattress out of the back of the wagon and leaned it against the side with the other. She sighed. One whole day to rest. Fort Bridger should have supplies, too, that they sorely needed.

"I don't like for you to have to do everything." Mama eased her swollen body into the rocker.

Katie looked at her mother who was well into her ninth month. "Just rest, Mama. I don't want to lose you, too."

Mama placed a hand on her well-rounded stomach. She leaned back and closed her eyes so Katie climbed into the wagon and straightened things that had been used recently. The work kept her from thinking about the inner upheaval she felt almost continually since her father's death. Mama's Bible drew her like a moth to a flame. Yet with each reading her discontent intensified along with the knowledge that something was lacking in her life.

~*~

After Fort Bridger, the company turned northwest toward Fort Hall. With each day that passed, Katie's concern for her mother grew as her time drew near. The only time she left her mother's side was when she had to drive the cattle. As a result, her nerves were on edge most of the time so that she snapped at Suzy or Tommy with the least provocation.

Finally Mama spoke to her about it. "Katie, would you like to tell me what is wrong."

Katie looked up from the water she had just sloshed when she set it down in haste. "I don't know what you're talking about."

"Come sit beside me and let's talk."

Katie sank to the ground at her mother's feet, unsure if she wanted this conversation. What good would it do? Only stir up more confusion in her mind.

Mama stroked her hair with a loving hand. "I know it's been hard. So many lives lost and we still aren't there. Yet God has been good to us, too. When others died of mountain fever, God allowed us to keep Suzy. Can you tell me what's troubling you?"

Tears welled in Katie's eyes as she felt her mother's gentle hand against her head. "I hurt so bad right here." She placed her hand over her heart. "I'm worried about you and the baby. I feel so mixed up inside. I don't know what to do, Mama."

"Honey, God is calling you to Him."

Katie looked up through her tears. "But, Mama, God doesn't want me."

Mama's hand stilled. "What do you mean?"

"I was so angry with Dad. I hated him for taking our home away from us. I hated him for making you travel when you should be in Missouri in your house. It was your farm, Mama, not his. And I hated him for dying. But that doesn't matter now, does it? Because he's gone. He's gone and I can't tell him I'm sorry." Her voice broke, and she swallowed hard against the tears choking her. "I can't tell him I forgive him. And I hate him for that, too."

"No, you can't tell Dad, but you can tell God." Mama's hand moved to again stroke Katie's hair.

"A ray of hope touched Katie's heart. "Would that help?"

Mama smiled. "Yes, it would help. Jesus said in Matthew: 'Come unto me, all ye that labor and are heavy laden and I will give you rest.' That's all you have to do. Just come to Jesus in prayer. He has told us in His word, "If we confess our sins, He is faithful and just to forgive our sins.' All you have to do is tell Jesus you are sorry, ask Him to forgive you, then believe that He has."

Katie looked up at her mother with wide eyes. "That's all?"

"Yes, darling, that is all."

Katie was tired of the hate. She was tired of the guilt. What would it hurt to do as Mama's suggested? It might even help.

With faith as of a small child, she bowed her head. "I'm so sorry, Jesus."

Those few words released a flood of tears. "Please forgive me. Take this anger away and give me peace."

Katie's simple prayer flowed as she opened her heart and released the restlessness she'd carried for too long. Peace spread through her as balm to her soul. She lifted her head. "Thank you, Mama. I love you so very much."

Tears glistened in Mama's eyes. "Oh, Katie, you have made me very happy. I love you, and I'm so proud of you."

That night Katie went to sleep almost as soon as she settled down and slept peacefully until the wee hours of the morning when she awoke to a sound. Again she heard a low moan, as someone in pain.

Her eyes flew open all sleep gone. Mama!

Katie sat up in bed and reached across the wagon for her mother. She touched her forehead and felt the moisture of perspiration.

Mama's voice in the darkness sounded forced. "I had hoped we could wait until we got to Fort Hall, but I guess not."

Katie's heart thumped in her chest. "What do I do, Mama?"

"Wake Tommy and have him get Mrs. Bartlett, then come back. Tell him to hurry. My babies always come fast. And Katie, take Suzy to Mrs. Morgan."

"I will." Katie scrambled to the end of the wagon and climbed down. Tommy woke instantly when she touched his shoulder. "It's Mama's time. Go get Mrs. Bartlett."

Tommy didn't speak, but hurried off to get the midwife.

Katie climbed back into the wagon and pulled Susanna from her bed. She laid her still sleeping little sister at the back end and climbed down before picking her back up. Her heart raced. What if Mama had the baby before she could get back. She said to hurry, but she'd have to wake Mrs. Morgan and that would take time.

"Katie, I'm here." Rachel's voice came from the darkness between the wagons.

"Oh, thank you, Lord." Katie handed her little sister to Rachel.

"I've got her." Rachel's arms closed around the little girl. "You go on. She'll be fine."

With no more than a passing thought of how Rachel knew she needed help, Katie hurried back to her mother.

"Katie." Mary's voice sounded strange. "It's time. You'll have to help me."

The truth hit Katie as a physical blow. Never before had she heard fear in her mother's voice. A tremble moved through her body. "Mama, what do I do?"

"The baby's coming, Katie. I'm sorry. You'll have to take him now."

Katie saw the baby's head emerging. A sound of half groan, half scream came from her mother and sent chills down Katie's back. But she had no time to think as her little brother made his debut into the world and landed in her outstretched hands.

As his first cries split the air, Mrs. Bartlett stuck her head into the wagon before climbing up. "Let's get that cord tied off, then I'll check on your mama."

Katie turned with her brother in her arms. Her heart pounded so loud in her ears that she had trouble thinking. "Mrs. Bartlett, I am so glad to see you. I don't know what to do."

The older woman's grim expression did little to reassure her. She bustled about taking care of the baby and mother. Then she turned to Katie. "Send Tommy for Doctor Clark."

Katie didn't stop to question, but ran to the opening in back. Tommy and Rachel worked together to build up the campfire to warm some water. "Tommy, we need Dr. Clark quickly."

His head jerked up before he took off in a run.

Katie turned back and met Mrs. Bartlett who thrust the newborn, wrapped tightly in a blanket, into her arms. "I'll let you bathe him now."

Katie moved again to the end of the wagon and stepped out of the doctor's way as he climbed in. She crouched down near the opening. Surely the water hadn't had time to warm yet.

"Tommy. Rachel." She called softly to them. "Come see what I have. We have a little brother."

Both hurried to look. "Oh, Katie, he's beautiful." Rachel pulled the edge of the blanket back so they could see him in the predawn light.

Katie smiled. "He's not cleaned up yet. But you are right. He is beautiful."

"Boys can't be beautiful, but he looks fine." Tommy didn't smile. "How's Mama?"

Katie shook her head and glanced back where the doctor leaned over their mother. "I don't know. Dr. Clark's taking care of her."

"The water should be warm enough now." Rachel turned away to get a basin for the baby's first bath.

"Tommy, why is Rachel here?" Katie couldn't resist asking.

"I guess she wants to help." Tommy glanced toward Rachel. "Actually, I'm glad she's here."

"How'd she know we needed her?" Katie frowned, remembering. "I mean when I took Suzy to her mother, she met me before I even asked."

Tommy looked away with the hint of a grin. "Um, that's my fault. I got turned around and went to the Morgan's instead of the Bartletts."

Katie lifted her eyebrows.

Before she could speak, Rachel came with the basin of warm water and set it inside the wagon where Katie could reach it. Katie stared at it. "I don't know if I can do this."

"Don't look at me." Tommy stepped back with his hands up.

Rachel smiled at him before turning to Katie. "You can do it, Katie. I'm sure he's tougher than he looks. Just be gentle."

Katie took a deep breath and began. Her hand trembled and she jerked back when the baby let out a tiny cry and stiffened. As soon as he relaxed, she tried again and finished as quickly as she could then wrapped him in a clean blanket.

"Would you like to hold him?"

Rachel smiled and nodded, so she handed her precious brother to her friend. "I want to check on Mama."

She crept near where the doctor and midwife continued

working with her mother, but she didn't understand their concern. Mama appeared to be resting. "Doctor Clark, is something wrong?"

The doctor barely glanced her way. "She's hemorrhaging. Tell your brother to ask Mr. Colton to delay our start this morning by at least an hour."

Fear clutched Katie's heart as she turned to obey.

~*~

David Karl Donovan was so sweet. Katie couldn't have asked for an easier baby to care for. Mama was still weak and could do very little, so much of his care fell on her willing shoulders. Jason stopped by that evening to meet the new Donovan.

Katie had him wrapped in a blanket even though the evening was warm. She smiled at Jason when he knelt beside her rocking chair. "Do you want to hold him?"

"Sure."

Katie raised her eyebrows at his quick response. She stood and handed the baby to him. "Would you like to sit in the rocker?"

Jason held the small bundle as if he took care of babies all the time. He shook his head as he looked down at the sleeping baby. "That's all right. He doesn't weigh anything, does he?"

Katie shook her head. "Doctor Clark thought he weighed about seven pounds." She watched Jason cuddle her baby brother. Where had he learned to hold a baby? Most men she knew seemed awkward around babies. Even Tommy didn't want to hold him too often. But Jason acted like holding Davy was the most natural thing in the world.

"Have you been around babies much?" She couldn't resist asking.

Jason lifted his head. "No, why do you ask?"

"Because you seem so comfortable holding him."

Jason laughed. "I am comfortable. If you mean how do I know to support his head, that's easy. I've heard that baby's necks are floppy and I've seen other people hold babies. It doesn't take a genius to hold one, does it?"

"No, I guess not." Katie sat back in the rocker. "Jason."

His attention remained on the baby. "Hmm?"

"I wanted to tell you what happened to me the evening before Davy was born."

He looked at her as if searching her face for the answer.

"Mama prayed with me, and I accepted Jesus as my savior."

Jason's face lit up with his wide grin before he laughed. "Praise the Lord! You couldn't have told me anything better than that, Katie. I'm really glad to hear it."

Katie relaxed as Tommy joined them. She let the two men talk until bedtime without her input.

~*~

Jason sat and listened to Tommy talk about the journey ahead while his mind whirled. Katie had accepted the gift of salvation. They were no longer at odds in their beliefs. What did that mean for him? And for her?

"We're over halfway to Oregon now." Tommy's voice penetrated his thoughts. "I'll be glad when we can settle into our own homes."

"Yes, I think we all will." Jason let his gaze shift to Katie. She lifted a heavy iron skillet from the wagon. She was probably getting ready to fix supper.

He shifted to the rocker, still holding the baby. As he settled him in the crook of his arm and set the rocker moving, he let his imagination run wild as if Katie was fixing supper for him and Davy was their child.

"What are your plans once we get there?" Again Tommy broke into his musings.

Jason frowned. He'd better keep his mind on Tommy. Katie probably had her own plans made with Clay Monroe. If he kept pretending and wishing for things he couldn't have, he'd only get hurt. He shook his head. Tommy asked about his plans.

"I'd like to have my own place. Some land to make a living on." He looked down at the sleeping baby. "Maybe settle down and raise a family."

Tommy chuckled. "Looks like you'd be good at it the way you're holding Davy. I'm always afraid I'll drop him or hit his head against something. You look like you know what you're doing."

Jason grinned. "That's what Katie said. The truth is, I don't know much, but I figure a baby can't be that hard to hold. He doesn't weigh hardly anything."

"Yes, but that's what scares me. Because he's so little."

"You have a point." Jason felt the slight weight against his arm and found he liked it. A lot. Maybe someday he'd have a son as special as little Davy. If this child grew to be like his older brother, Karl, he'd be a very special child indeed.

Jason watched Katie mix something in a bowl. She'd make Clay a wonderful wife. His heart constricted at the thought, and he shifted his gaze to Tommy. "Yes, we're halfway there and that only means we have another long, hard journey ahead of us."

"That's true, but with God's help we'll make it." Tommy glanced toward the wagon.

Jason turned to see what had caught his attention. Suzy climbed down the ramp and ran toward them. "Hi, Jason."

She patted his knee. "Can I sit here with you and Davy?"

At Katie's sharp intake of air, Jason guessed she would protest her sister's forward behavior. He didn't mind, though. He liked Suzy. Before Katie spoke, he did. "Sure, climb on up. There's room for you and Davy both."

"Susanna Donovan," Katie called from the campfire. "You'd better thank Jason for being so nice to you."

Jason chuckled as Suzy gave him a sweet smile. "Thank you, Jason."

"You're welcome." Jason pulled her back against him.

Tommy shook his head. "I hope you find a good, Christian woman who shares your love of kids so you can fill up that farm you're planning on."

Jason grinned. He'd like nothing better. Only problem was, he'd already found the good, Christian woman he wanted. Too bad Monroe had beat him to her. It might be a long while before he found another to fill the space she'd left.

~*~

Katie rode behind the cattle as the train neared Fort Hall.

"Haw, move on there." She drove her cows into the valley where the other animals where gathering and breathed a sigh of relief. Another day behind the cattle ended so she could get back to Mama and Davy. Mama spent most of her time in the wagon caring for Davy or sleeping. She was better, but not well enough to do any work. If not for Rachel's help during the day, Katie didn't know what they would do.

Fort Hall stood between the Portneuf and Snake Rivers. Halfway to their new home. They couldn't get there soon enough for Katie. She turned Star loose and walked toward camp. Another train had also set up camp nearby, giving the appearance of small communities grouped together into one large city of white canvas homes. Hundreds of people milled about over the countryside. They would be stopping for a short rest according to Mr. Colton. Maybe Mama would regain her strength while they were here.

As soon as she found their wagon, she started building a fire then went in to check on her mother and the baby. "How are you feeling, Mama?"

Mama sat leaning against the side of the wagon with Davy in her arms. I'm fine, Katie. I just wish I could do more."

"We'll handle the work. You just get well."

Mama smiled. "I'm trying to, darling." She nodded toward a couple of bottles lying beside her. "I don't like giving you more work, but when you get some water boiling, could you put these in for several minutes and when they are clean, bring them to me?"

Katie took the baby bottles and several nipples from the bed and went outside without asking the questions that burned in her head. She had them boiling when Tommy stopped beside her. "Have you been in to see Mama?"

At her nod, he asked, "How is she?"

"I don't know, Tommy. She has so little strength." Katie looked up at him. "Actually, I'm worried about her. She asked me to boil these baby bottles and nipples for her. I'm sure she never used a bottle with the rest of us. I didn't even know she had any."

Tommy frowned and nodded. "I'll step in and see her

117

before I go up to the fort. With this mob here, there probably won't be a speck of anything left on the shelves, but at least I'll try."

Tommy moved to the wagon and disappeared inside.

Katie watched the water boil around the bottles and thought of her little brother. There was a special bond already forming between them that Katie attributed to the part she had played in his birth. She felt closer to him than she'd expected. She had been the first to see him and hold him. She smiled as she visualized his little round face topped by a thin layer of fuzzy, light orange-tinted hair. Already, he looked like Karl had as a baby.

She took the bottles out to cool and began preparing supper. As soon as she got some biscuits made she would check on Mama again.

Tommy came back from the fort carrying a slab of bacon and a sack of flour. "That was pretty much a waste of time."

Katie put them away. "Do you think you could ask the doctor to look at Mama?"

Tommy frowned. "Why? Is she worse?"

"I don't know. I looked in on her while ago and I think she's got fever. Something's wrong, Tommy. She won't admit it, but I think she hurts somewhere."

Tommy nodded and started back the way he'd come. "I saw Doctor Clark at the storehouse. I'll go get him."

As soon as Katie saw Tommy and Dr. Clark coming, she picked up the baby and told Susanna to follow her. She sat with the baby cuddled close in her arms and waited while the doctor entered the wagon.

Susanna pressed close to Katie's side, her brown eyes wide and serious. "Katie, is Mama going to Heaven with Daddy and Karl?"

Katie's breath caught in her throat. She looked over Susanna's head to Tommy. What could she say?

Tommy knelt beside his little sister. He put his arms around her, turning her to face him. "Suzy, we don't know if Mama is leaving us. But we want you to know if she does, we'll take very good care of you. You do know that, don't you?"

Susanna nodded even as tears sparkled in her eyes. Katie blinked to keep her own in check as her little sister began to sob. "I don't want Mama to go away. I want her to stay here with me."

Tommy held her close. "I don't want her to go either, Suzy, but I know if she does, she'll be happy. God's home is much nicer than it is here, and someday if we love Him we'll all get to go there, too."

Susanna pulled away from Tommy and looked into his face. "I guess Daddy and Karl miss Mama, don't they?"

Tommy nodded. "I'm sure they do."

The doctor climbed from the wagon, and Tommy rose to meet him. "Doctor Clark, is she . . . ?"

The older man shook his head. "She's got a fever. There's infection inside. We'll fight it as best we can, but I don't know—I just don't know. I'm sorry, kids."

When he left, Katie looked at Tommy. "I keep remembering what Mama told us when we were in Independence after she sold her organ about this move being hardest on us. Somehow she must have known. I'm glad we're both serving the Lord now. We need Him so much."

"Tommy." Jason strode into their camp and glanced briefly at her before turning to Tommy. "Is there anything I can do to help?"

"What do you have in mind?" Tommy frowned.

Jason rubbed the back of his neck. "I saw the doctor just now and know your mother isn't well. I figured that's putting a lot off on Katie and thought maybe I could help out some."

Katie rocked the baby and watched Jason. He still hadn't spoken to her although he seemed to have no trouble talking about her.

Tommy nodded. "All right, I'm listening."

"I don't need to drive the Taylor's wagon. Pa Taylor can do it himself. That will leave me free to ride herd on your cattle. What do you say? Will you let me help you out like a Christian brother should?"

A slow grin spread across Tommy's face, and he held out his hand for Jason to shake. "When you put it that way, how can

I refuse?"

"What about me?" Katie straightened. "Do I have a say in any of this?"

Both men turned to look at her as if just realizing she was there. Tommy frowned at her. "Katie, Jason offered to help us out. I don't see how we can refuse because, the truth be known, we need it."

"I know that, Tommy." Katie looked at Jason although she still talked to her brother. "I appreciate the offer of help from Mr. Barnett, but since I'm the one who will benefit most from this help, I'd like to at least be included in the decision."

"We'll all benefit, Katie." Tommy sounded tired. "You'll not have to work so hard, Mama will get better care, and I can stop worrying so much about you all."

Katie felt the reprimand for her pettiness and was instantly sorry, but Jason spoke first. "I apologize, Katie. It was not my intention to ignore you. I just felt that Tommy, as head of the house now, would be the one to speak to."

Katie looked into the sky blue eyes that always made her feel as if her very thoughts were known. Her heart thumped loud in the silence before she spoke.

"You were right, Jason. Thank you for what you're doing. We are worried about Mama. Maybe if I'm here with her all the time, she'll get better."

Jason's smile warmed Katie's heart. "That's what I'm hoping for, too. The Taylors and I have been praying for her. I know God is with her. I don't think I've ever met a godlier woman than your mother."

Katie stayed close to her mother for the next few days. Some days she felt better than others. One day when they were halfway between Fort Hall and Fort Boise, she stayed up most of the day and took care of Davy without help. That afternoon, Katie left her and Tommy with the two small children while she walked with Rachel to the creek.

The girls filled their buckets of water and set them aside while they fell back against the creek bank to rest before starting back to camp. Katie looked up at the white clouds floating above and sighed.

"Have you ever tried to find shapes in the clouds?"

Rachel laughed. "Yes, and I see one now. There's an alligator over there."

"An alligator!" Katie glanced at her friend before pointing to another place in the sky. "You can see alligators if you want, but I see a huge ear of corn covered with yellow butter."

Rachel's laughter was contagious and soon Katie joined in. "I should have known you would see food. As tiny as you are, that seems to be your favorite subject."

"Katie."

The girls were still laughing when someone called Katie's name. She sat up and saw Rachel's brother running toward them.

"Katie, Tommy sent me for you. He says to hurry. Your mother is worse."

"She was better today." Katie scrambled to her feet. "How could she be worse?"

"That's what Tommy said." Daniel repeated his message. "Don't worry about your water. I'll bring it to you."

Chapter 14

*K*atie gathered her skirt and ran toward camp. When she got to the wagon, she climbed in and found Tommy and Susanna kneeling beside the bed where their mother lay. She had lost so much weight; the quilt barely rose off the bed over her body. Her baby slept beside her, snuggled in the crook of her arm.

Katie knelt by Tommy and took her mother's hand. "Mama, what can I do?"

Mama smiled and shook her head. "I'll be all right in a while. I'm going home."

As if Mama's words were a heavy hand pushing against her chest, Katie moved backward. "No, Mama, please don't say that. We need you here."

Tommy's arm slipped around Katie's shoulders. He gave comfort even while tears streamed down his face. Susanna began crying, and he pulled her close, too.

Mama's gaze rested on Katie. "No, you don't need me. Children, you have Someone now who is able to take care of you much better than I can. He will see you through whatever comes."

Her eyes drifted closed. "I must tell you some things. The little ones need you." She stirred, looking from Tommy to Katie. "You will marry soon and begin homes of your own. Suzy must be allowed to choose where she wants to live. Please, promise me you will let her."

Tommy nodded. "We will, Mama."

"David needs a mother most right now." Mama turned to spear Katie with her gaze. "I want you to be his mother. Will you do that for me?"

Tears blurred Katie's eyes, and she didn't trust her voice, but she managed to whisper. "I will."

Mama smiled. "You'll be a good mother."

Then she turned to Tommy. "My Bible is for you all to read and study, but Tommy, I want you to keep it as your own. The answers to life's problems are in its pages. Please, read it to Suzy and Davy."

Next she slipped her wedding band easily from her thin finger and placed it in Tommy's hand. "I want you to have this."

A look of bewilderment crossed his face as he took the wide, plain, gold band from her hand.

"It's a new country you're going to. You need a good wife to help you. Promise me you'll find a Christian girl."

Tommy looked steadily at his mother. "I promise. I wouldn't want any other now."

A faint smile touched Mama's face. "If she will, I'd like for her to wear my ring."

Tommy looked at the ring in his hand. "I'll try my best to find a wife worthy of the honor you've given her."

Mama touched Tommy's hand that held the ring. "Remember, Son, I'm not perfect and neither will she be."

She took Katie's hand and placed it beside Tommy's then covered theirs with her hand. "Pray for God to show you who He wants to be your companions. Both of you are babes in Christ. My heart is so blessed that you have turned to God. Now I can go home knowing you will continue living for Him and guiding the two little ones in the right way. Remember, as your lives have been influenced by those who went before you, so will you touch the lives of those who follow."

Mama's eyes closed, and her hand relaxed. "I'm tired now."

Katie held back the sob that threatened to escape and reached for her baby brother. She had been right in thinking he was more than a brother to her. Someday he would also be her son.

Mary Donovan died in her sleep that night. When Katie found her the next morning she held Davy and Susanna and cried with them until she had no more tears. Then she washed her face and went to find Tommy.

The funeral was held just before they pulled the wagons out for another day's travel. Katie stood beside her mother's grave and held the baby. She felt a comforting presence warm her heart as she stood there and knew it was God who strengthened her in her grief. This funeral seemed so different from the others. How had she ever managed to live before without God's uplifting help?

Then someone stepped close to her and without looking, she knew it was Jason. "I want you to know I'm here for you anytime you need me. If there's anything I can do, just let me know."

She turned to meet his concern. "Jason you are already driving the cows for me."

"Yes, and I intend to keep doing that." He grinned. "Actually, I enjoy it."

"I'm glad someone does."

He touched the baby's tiny hand. Surprise crossed his face as the tiny, soft fist closed around his large, work-roughened finger. "Well, look at that. Does that mean he likes me?"

Katie shook her head. "I'm sure he likes you, but to be honest, all babies grab whatever is placed in their hands."

Jason slid his finger free. "What I know about babies wouldn't fill a teaspoon. Except how to hold them." He grinned. "Maybe I could visit young Mr. Donovan from time to time so he can teach me a few things. Would that be all right?"

He looked hopefully from Katie to Tommy who was approaching with Susanna clinging to his hand.

Tommy nodded. "You're welcome anytime. Why don't you stop by tonight? Rachel said she missed the evenings we spent reading the Bible by the campfire before Mama got sick. I think Mama would want us to start again. How about it, Katie? Why don't you invite Rachel, too?"

Katie nodded. "All right, I will."

Jason turned away promising to see them later that evening, and Katie walked with Tommy back to their wagon. When they reached camp, Tommy let out a huff of air and leaned his shoulder against the wagon. "Three hundred more miles. Do you reckon any of us will be left to enter our

'Promised Land'?"

Katie searched Tommy's face and saw tension that shouldn't be there. The brunt of the responsibility for their remaining family had already settled on his young shoulders. He looked tired—and older. There was maturity about him she hadn't noticed before. She straightened her own shoulders and lifted her chin. She would do what she could to share that responsibility.

"We'll make it, Tommy, you'll see. Only three hundred miles more? Just think how far we've come already and now that we're both serving the Lord, we have help we didn't have before."

~*~

Jason headed back to the Taylor's camp. He wanted to take Katie in his arms and soothe her. He'd been with her through the other times when Karl drowned and her father was shot, but this time was different. She didn't need him, and he felt the loss while he rejoiced in her trust in God. Katie had changed. More than he'd dreamed was possible.

Ma Taylor was putting things away, getting ready to head out when he walked up behind her. What would he do if he lost either of the Taylors? He'd taken them for granted most of his life when he shouldn't have. They were young enough now, only in their upper forties, but each day that passed brought them closer to the day they'd be taken from him. His heart constricted at the thought.

"Hey, Ma." He called out as he approached. "Is there anything I can help you with?"

She turned with a laugh and covered her heart with her hand. "You startled me, Jason. I didn't know you were anywhere about. No, there's not much to do."

"No heavy loads to lift, huh?" He grinned at her.

She patted his arm. "Not a one."

Her smile faded. "How are the kids taking this latest loss?"

"Better than I expected. They've been through a lot on this journey, but they aren't the same as when they started out. Katie has changed so much." He shook his head. "She doesn't need—"

Ma folded her arms and looked at him. "She doesn't need what, Jason? You? She has the Lord to see her through life's hurts now, and you're feeling just a bit left out. Is that it?"

Jason took a deep breath and let it ease out. Ma was right. He was feeling a little sorry for himself. He'd gone up to Katie earlier, hoping to be a comfort to her. Well, maybe he had been, but she hadn't really needed him. When Clay hadn't stood with Katie during the funeral, he'd entertained the idea he might have a chance with her, but did he? He didn't know.

"I need to go saddle Star. We've got cattle to move." He turned away from Ma.

As he walked away, she called out. "Don't give up too easily, Jason. Sometimes what's hardest to win is the most worthwhile."

He tried to ignore her, but the thought she planted in his mind stayed with him all through the long day as he rode Star and kept the Donovan's cattle in line. By the time camp was made that night, he welcomed the chance to rest.

After seeing that the animals were taken care of for the night, Jason walked back to camp and ate supper with Ma and Pa. He set his plate aside and stood. "Do you need water?"

"No." Ma shook her head while a faint smiled played around her lips. "I've got some already heating. Of course, if you want to do the dishes for me . . ."

"Sure, I can do that." He turned and picked up his plate.

Ma laughed. "No, you don't. I'll take care of the dishes. You go on and check on the Donovans. Let me know if there's anything they need."

"All right. I forgot to tell you Tommy wants to continue the Bible readings his mother started. They'll be doing that here in a few minutes if you want to join in."

Ma and Pa shared a look. Jason watched them communicate without words and envied them the closeness they shared. That's what he wanted. Love and companionship with a special woman who shared his beliefs and dreams. If Ma and Pa Taylor ever fought he didn't know about it. Yet their love for each other was evident in each look and touch they shared. He wasn't surprised when Pa turned to him and nodded.

126

"Sure, we'd like to join the group tonight. Mrs. Donovan was a good woman. In her quiet way, she touched more lives than she realized. Looks like her kids are following in her footsteps now."

~*~

Jason sat on the ground with his arm resting across his bent knee. Susanna sat on his other leg, leaning against his chest. He liked having her there, although Katie had protested. She should know by now how much he enjoyed little Suzy's attention. Tonight, the little girl needed to be held. She hadn't said much, but he could tell she missed her mother. In fact, her quiet spoke of her grief louder than words would have. His heart broke for her and for her big sister and brother. They were all hurting. Still, they wanted to have the Bible reading tonight.

Tommy sat on a wooden barrel he'd pulled from the wagon. He held his mother's Bible in his hands. "Mama loved the Psalms." His voice broke. He swallowed before going on. "When anything happened, good or bad, she read the 23rd Psalm. I'd like to read Mama's favorite scripture tonight. Maybe, as she sings praise to the Lord, she'll stop for a few minutes to listen and be assured that we're all right."

Jason's heart felt heavy for his friends. He glanced at Katie sitting beside him with the baby cradled in her arms. She looked so maternal. The image of her and Davy sank deep into his mind and heart. His arm tightened around Susanna. What would happen to them? To Katie, Susanna, and Davy? Tommy would be all right. He'd take care of himself, but what could Katie do with two small children? She'd have to marry or expect Tommy to support them. Clay wasn't there tonight and hadn't been evident for some time. If he wanted to marry Katie, now would be the best time to step forward. Maybe he didn't. Some men became scarce when the good times stopped. Clay might be one of those men.

"The Lord is my shepherd, I shall not want." Tommy's voice rang out loud and clear.

Jason concentrated on his friend's voice and let the ancient words of David ring true for his life.

"He leadeth me in the paths of righteousness for His name

sake." Jason let that thought sink deep into his soul. *Lord, lead me in Your paths, in the paths of righteousness. For Your name's sake. Amen.*

~*~

Katie bowed her head for Tommy's closing prayer. Mama had always prayed after she finished a Bible reading. Tommy wanted to continue the tradition she'd started. How strange to think of the changes that had occurred in the last few months. When they started on the trail, she and Tommy found every excuse they could to avoid Mama's Bible readings. Now look at them. Not only willing participants, but eager to continue and even lead. Mama would be happy to see how many came tonight to listen to God's word. Unless she'd missed someone, there were seventeen present.

Katie stood with Davy on one arm while she shook hands with those who had joined them. Mr. and Mrs. Bartlett and their children left first.

"Time to get these kids to bed." Mrs. Bartlett laughed and nudged her sleepy daughter forward.

"I'm glad you came." Katie smiled at the little girl's droopy eyes.

"Let us know when you do this again. We'll be back if we're still welcome."

"Oh, you certainly are." Katie glanced toward Tommy who was talking to Mr. Taylor. "I think Tommy wants to have a reading at least twice a week. We'll let you know."

"Katie," Rachel called to her. "We're going on, but I'll see you tomorrow."

"Okay." Katie waved at Rachel, her parents, and her brother, Daniel.

As they left, she turned to Mrs. Taylor who gave her a warm hug. "This is wonderful what you kids are doing."

"Thank you. I'm so glad you came." Katie sensed Jason standing just behind her. She glanced over her shoulder and saw he held Susanna. She appeared to be asleep. He'd latched onto her as if she were his little sister instead of a nuisance.

"Well, I see Mr. Taylor's ready to go now. I hope you continue the readings. Your mother would approve. She was a wonderful woman." Mrs. Taylor started away.

Katie called after her, "Thank you."

Mrs. Taylor waved, so Katie turned to Jason. "Are you ready to put that burden down?"

Jason grinned. "She isn't a burden, but yeah, she probably needs to be in bed. Do you have a place ready for her?"

"Oh, yes, I knew this would happen so her bed's ready. Can you carry her inside?"

"Sure."

Katie headed toward the wagon and climbed up the ramp with Davy held close to her. He was sleeping, too, but she didn't want to lay him down. Somehow, holding him tonight while Tommy read from the Bible brought Mama closer. She wasn't ready to give up that comfort.

Jason lay Susanna down and pulled her shoes off as if he took care of children every day. "Where do you put these?"

Katie took the shoes from his hand. "You never cease to amaze me."

She shook her head and set them on a box then moved to the back and stepped out onto the ramp. Jason took her arm to help her down then followed. He stood and looked down at her, searching her face as if he expected to find something that wasn't there. She didn't know what he looked for, but his gaze sent shivers down her back that was not at all unpleasant. She felt drawn toward him in a way becoming too familiar. Probably because of his willingness to help. Who wouldn't appreciate that?

"Will you be all right, Katie?" His voice sounded low and caressing.

She nodded. "Yes, we'll be fine. Don't worry about us. You're doing so much more than you should to help us now."

"Not too much." Jason frowned.

"But enough." Tommy stepped up beside Katie. "We owe you a lot, but with God's help, we'll get to Oregon."

Jason shifted to look at Tommy. "I know that's true. If there's anything you need, though, let me know."

"We will." Tommy leaned against the wagon. "The same goes for you. If you folks need our help, just let us know."

"Fair enough." Jason stepped back. "I'll get out of your way now. Good service, Tommy. I enjoyed being here."

"Thanks."

Jason turned and walked away. Katie watched until he went past the next wagon out of her sight.

"Tommy." Mr. Colton strode toward them with a young couple following close behind. Katie recognized the Parkers, whose baby son lay in an unmarked grave several hundred miles behind. What could they want?

Tommy pushed away from the wagon and faced the wagon master.

Mr. Colton cleared his throat and gave a brisk nod. "Tommy, Katie, we want to say how sorry we are about the loss of your mother. She was a fine lady. I'm sure everyone who met her would say so."

"Thank you, sir." Tommy nodded. "We appreciate that."

Mr. Colton glanced toward the Parkers. "You know Mr. and Mrs. Parker."

Again Tommy nodded.

"Well, there's no reason to beat around the bush." Mr. Colton coughed. "If you'll remember, the Parkers here lost their little boy, and they've come with the offer to take your baby brother so he can be cared for properly. They'd like to take him and raise him as their own son."

Chapter 15

Katie gasped and clutched Davy close. Her knees buckled and she sucked in a sharp breath. She couldn't hear the man's voice for the pounding of her heart. Why wouldn't her legs let her take Davy and run away from these people? She stared at the two men and woman who smiled as if their outrageous statement made sense. They expected her to gladly hand over part of her family—part of her heart.

Through the roaring in her head, she heard Tommy's calm voice. "I know you mean well and we do appreciate your thoughtfulness, but we promised our mother we'd take care of him."

Mrs. Parker smiled as if Tommy were a child. "Of course. And it would be taking care of him if you let me have him."

Tommy shook his head. "No, she meant for us to stay together."

Mr. Parker frowned. "You're just kids. A baby needs a mother."

The audacity of the Parkers and Mr. Colton stirred embers of fire in Katie's heart and loosed her tongue. She stepped forward rather than back. *Lord, help us.* Her voice rang out with strength. "Mr. Colton, our mother's dying request was that I become Davy's mother. She trusted me, and with God's help I will honor her trust. We are keeping our brother. Letting you take him would be like another death. Don't you think we've had enough deaths in our family?"

She didn't bother waiting for their answer. All three stood with their mouths open, probably shocked that she and Tommy dared defy them. She turned away and climbed the ramp into the wagon, Davy still held close. Inside, a tremble began and spread to her hands so much she feared she might drop her sweet baby. She felt her way carefully to his small bed and laid him in it then sat beside Susanna in the dark. With her head bowed, she covered her face with her hands while silent tears ran down her cheeks. Would the nightmare of this journey ever end?

"All right." Mr. Parker's voice came through the thin wall of canvas. "We'll leave it at that for now, but if we find out that baby's not getting proper care, we'll be back to get him."

There were footsteps and silence then Mr. Colton's gruff voice. "You kids think you can make it?"

Tommy answered, "Don't worry about us. We'll be fine."

"All right, but if it gets too hard, you let me know. There are plenty of women on this train that can help you with that baby."

"I'll help. They won't need anyone else." Katie's head jerked up at the sound of Rachel's gentle voice outside. Tears again filled her eyes. Rachel was not a do-gooder, but a true friend. *Thank you, Lord.*

After a short stretch of silence, Mr. Colton said, "That's fine, but I'd be mighty careful if I were you and I wanted to keep that baby. The Parkers'll be watching you like a hawk."

"Yes, sir." Tommy said. "We appreciate your advice, but like I said, I'm sure we'll get along fine."

Katie slipped to the end of the wagon and peeked out. Mr. Colton turned and walked away. The Parkers must have left earlier. "Rachel. Are you really going to ride with us and help?"

Rachel stepped closer to Katie. "I overheard what was going on, and I couldn't stand by and not offer. Yes, I'd love to if you don't mind."

"I certainly don't. Do you mind, Tommy?"

Tommy had turned away and now stopped to look at his sister. "Mind? Oh, you mean Rachel's help." He grinned at Rachel. "I can't imagine anyone turning down an honest offer of help."

Rachel's face grew rosy as she met Tommy's grin. She smiled. "In that case I'd better make sure my offer is honest by asking my parents if it's all right with them."

She spun away with a wave. "I'll be back early in the

morning. I know they'll say yes."

~*~

Rachel's help had to have been ordered by God. Katie thanked God daily for sending her. How did one woman handle two children day in and day out? Yet most raised several more than that and made it look easy. She looked up at the overcast sky and sighed. The weather had been dismal and threatening for several days.

"Think it'll rain?" Rachel carried the blanket-wrapped baby to Mama's rocking chair and sat down with him. "I hope the dampness in the air doesn't hurt little Davy."

Tommy returned from staking the oxen with the other animals. He stopped by Rachel and touched the blanket, smoothing it away from Davy's face. "It won't hurt him. He's never been in a house, so he's used to the changes of the weather. If we keep him dry and warm, he'll be fine."

"How long are we staying here?" Katie looked toward Fort Boise. The high adobe walls protected an oasis in the harsh land they were traveling through. The gate was open, welcoming, as if inviting the weary travelers to come and take from the abundant supplies inside. Only, that wasn't the case. They'd been able to purchase fish, a few beans, and very little flour and bacon.

Tommy looked at the fort and shook his head. "Only overnight. Mr. Colton wants to beat the rain to the Snake River crossing."

Katie cringed at the thought of another river crossing. She knelt to add a stick to the fire.

Tommy turned and walked away, but Rachel must have noticed. "It'll be all right, Katie. We've made it across enough rivers that the men are getting experienced. You'll see, we'll soon be on the other side."

Katie nodded and tried to smile. Her fear showed a lack of trust that she desperately wanted to overcome. She sighed. "I know. I've been hoping the fear would go away, but ever since Karl's death, I've fought it."

"Maybe we should make your fear a matter of prayer." Rachel smoothed Susanna's hair as the little girl snuggled close.

"Would you like to sit on my lap with Davy?"

Susanna's braid bounced with her nod, and Rachel pulled her up before turning back to Katie. "Tonight at Bible study, we can ask the others to pray if that's all right with you."

Katie shrugged and hung the kettle of beans she'd been soaking over the fire. "I don't suppose it's a secret so I might as well swallow my pride and ask for help. Do you think we'll have a good crowd tonight?"

"Of course, we will." Rachel laughed. "I counted fifty in attendance last week. Your brother is getting a reputation you know."

"I think you're right." Katie stirred the ingredients for cornbread. She always tried to make extra so it would last through breakfast and lunch the next day. "Did you know Clay was there? Not taking part, but I saw him standing on the edge of the crowd listening."

"Yes, I saw him. He left before the closing prayer. Still, I believe he gained from being there. I know I did." Rachel shifted Susanna and turned to face Katie. "He's stopped coming over here, hasn't he? I mean isn't pursuing your hand—oh, don't answer that. It's none of my business."

A soft laugh rushed from Katie's lips as she poured the batter into her iron skillet. "It's all right, Rachel. He's lost interest in me, and that's fine. As far as I know, Clay isn't a Christian. Even if he were, I don't think he'd be happy with me. A man who thinks first of himself might get an earful after a while."

Rachel laughed. "I have a feeling you're right, you wouldn't put up with that long, and you shouldn't. It's better you know what he's like now than after it's too late."

"I agree, but that doesn't stop me from praying for him. He needs the Lord just as we all do."

~*~

"Does anyone have something you'd like prayer for?" Tommy stood before another large group that night.

Katie sat next to Jason with Davy held close in her lap. Susanna, as usual, clung to Jason. Rachel stirred beside Katie and held up her hand. When Tommy nodded to her, she stood.

"I'm sure most of us are frightened by the river crossings. We are facing another soon. Katie has asked that we pray for her and all who, like her, struggle with this fear. Let's pray we can fully trust God to take us safely across."

Many murmured their agreement. Other requests were given before Tommy bowed his head. "Father God, we come before You with humble hearts. The Snake River lies before us, and while it isn't the roughest we've crossed, we have learned that all rivers pose danger and threat of loss. Be with us . . ."

The warmth of Jason's touch on her hand drew Katie's attention toward him although she didn't turn his way. When the prayer ended, he gave her hand a quick squeeze then sat back as if he'd not touched her. But his warmth enveloped her heart. She turned just enough to let him see her smile and to receive one.

~*~

Jason couldn't fully concentrate on Tommy's comments with Katie sitting so close. He'd become used to seeing her with Davy in her arms. The baby was growing, thriving in her care as he'd expected. She made a wonderful mother.

Susanna squirmed on his lap, and he bent to whisper in her ear. "Let's sit still so everyone can hear what Tommy has to say."

The little girl twisted to look up into his face. A pout pushed out her lower lip. "I don't want to."

Her words were soft, but he heard the rebellion in them. He shook his head at her. "Don't tell me that. You'll sit still if you want me to play a game with you after the meeting."

Her eyes grew large as she stared into his. "With my dolly?"

Her dolly? Jason swallowed. What had he gotten himself into now? He glanced toward Katie. Their whispering had caught her attention, and amusement danced in her emerald eyes. She'd heard. He squared his shoulders and turned back to Suzy. "All right, but only for a while before you and your dolly go to bed."

Susanna grinned and leaned back against him, sitting quietly once more.

Jason lifted his eyebrows at Katie. Parenting wasn't so hard. Playing for a few minutes with a five-year-old couldn't be that bad, even if the idea of playing with a doll did seem foreign to him. Katie probably expected him to refuse.

A smile hovered over her lips and danced in her eyes. He'd been captivated by the green in her eyes that first day back in Independence when he helped build a fire for her and her mother. He'd fallen in love with her when she'd faced one hurt after another, and that love had grown along with her faith until she'd accepted God's love. If only he could win her love, he'd ask her to marry him. He wanted to help her raise Susanna and Davy.

Katie looked away, breaking the connection between them. Jason's gaze slid over the gathering until he spotted Clay standing in the shadows apart, yet within the range of Tommy's voice.

"'Let not your heart be troubled: ye believe in God, believe also in me. In my Father's house are many mansions, if it were not so, I would have told you. I go to prepare a place for you.'" Tommy paused and looked at those gathered in a semi-circle around him. "Folks, do you understand what Jesus is saying here? He's giving us all we need to make heaven our home. He's telling us not to worry, but to trust Him. Believe in Him just as we believe in God. He's getting our mansion ready now."

Clay seemed to be listening intently. *Lord, bring the truth alive in Clay's heart. In the hearts of any within hearing who need to accept your gift of eternal life. Bless each one here tonight and draw us close to You.*

If Clay accepted the Lord, he might come back to Katie. Jason cringed at the thought, but couldn't shake it from his mind. If she preferred Clay, there would be nothing he could do about it. He needed to accept the truth. Clay had been Katie's first choice. His heart sank. What was he thinking? He'd never been in the running because Clay had been her only choice.

As Tommy finished reading and commenting on the fourteenth chapter of John, he closed his Bible and looked around. "I feel there are some here tonight who need to believe in Jesus. Not only that Jesus exists, but that He is the only way to heaven. He is God. He's our savior and He's waiting for you to say, 'Lord, I believe. Forgive me for my unbelief and my willful neglect of the sacrifice You made for my salvation.'"

From the corner of his eye, Jason saw Clay spin on his heel and leave. His heart sank. He might not want Clay and Katie back together, but he would rejoice in welcoming a new Christian brother. *Lord, speak to his heart. Draw him to You.*

As others moved forward and knelt to pray, Jason looked down at Susanna. Her eyes were closed. Her lips parted as a soft breath escaped. He met Katie's amused gaze with a grin. "Reckon I don't get to play dolly tonight?"

"Don't gloat too much. She'll remember tomorrow as soon as she wakes up."

He shrugged. "I promised so I'll do it as soon as I can."

Tomorrow he had to move cattle and try to coax more milk from a cow that gave less every day. Katie's eyes seemed to hold admiration for him now, but would they if she knew the next problem they faced might affect Davy?

Chapter 16

"*W*ell, what do you think? Is God faithful?" Rachel laughed with her face lifted toward the warming sun. She grabbed Susanna's hand. "Let's skip, Suzy. The rain has ended and the sun feels so wonderful this morning. We've just crossed another river without mishap."

Katie smiled as Susanna tried to keep up with Rachel's skips. She called out to her friend. "Yes, as you well know. God is always faithful." She kissed Davy's soft covering of hair as the other two stopped and waited for her to catch up. "I believe that was the easiest crossing we've had yet."

"Pa says we're getting close." Rachel swung Susanna around, holding both her hands. "We'll make camp near the Blue Mountains tonight."

Susanna giggled and jumped in place when they stopped. "Do it again, Rachel."

Rachel knelt to Susanna's level with her arm around her shoulders and pointed. "Look at them, Suzy. They are so big. They'll stand watch over us while we sleep tonight."

Susanna shook her head. "Mountains can't watch us, Rachel."

Rachel laughed. "I guess my attempt at being poetic fell short. No, Suzy, mountains can't watch us, but God can. And He will, just like He did when we crossed the Snake River."

She turned to look at Katie. "Have you heard anything more from the Parkers?"

Fear, far too familiar, thrust through Katie's heart at the mention of the Parkers. She shivered. "Other than when I catch them staring at me, you mean? Thankfully, no."

Davy was six weeks old now and seemed unaffected by the hard trail. She cradled his chubby, little body and looked down into his bright, alert gaze. He was always so happy, content to lie in his crib and watch any activity going on around him when he wasn't asleep. He cried only when he was hungry or needed a diaper change. But never for long. She saw to that. She didn't want the Parkers to hear him and show up at their wagon again.

Katie lifted her gaze toward the cloud of dust moving alongside the train. Men on horseback moved the extra animals and Jason was somewhere among them, faithfully taking care of their cattle. He even milked the cows. A frown creased her forehead. Lately, he'd been getting less milk than usual. If only the cows could be allowed to stop for a few days and graze, maybe it would help. Although grass covered the valley where they walked, it didn't seem to be enough for the cows to produce milk. This continual moving was hard on everyone.

As if reading her thoughts, Rachel said, "Don't worry, Katie. God will supply milk for Davy. I know there hasn't been enough for anyone else the last few days, but he hasn't gone without yet."

"Suzy didn't get any milk yesterday." Katie sighed. "I can't seem to stop thinking about what may happen if all the cows go dry. Last night, Jason said he's only milking one of them now. The others have already given out. The Parkers will take Davy if they find out about this."

Rachel's silence sounded loud in Katie's heart. If only someone would tell her what to do. She missed her mother more every day. Mama would have known how to take care of Davy.

~*~

Katie hooked the pot of soup over the fire and stepped back. She turned as Jason strode across the grass.

"Hi." He took off his hat and wiped sweat and grime from his forehead. "Is Tommy here?"

"He just took the oxen to the holding pen. He should be back any minute." Something was wrong. The worry in Jason's eyes spoke for him. "What is it? What's happened?"

Jason took a deep breath and let it out. "It's the cows. I thought maybe I should tell Tommy first."

Katie covered her chest with her hand to ease the stab of fear his words brought. "Jason Barnett, you tell me what it is."

She twirled away. "Oh, forget it. I already know. You didn't get any milk tonight, did you?"

Katie didn't want Jason to see her cry. The very thing she feared had happened. What would they do now? Davy had to have milk to live. The Parkers would take him for sure.

"Katie, I'm sorry." Jason touched her shoulders and pulled her back against his chest. His breath brushed her ear. "I don't know what else to do. I tried. I really did."

Katie turned and stepped back to face him. He dropped his hands, but she laid a hand on his arm. "I know, Jason. I'm not blaming you. I feel so helpless. We have to do something, or we'll lose Davy."

"What's going on?" Tommy hurried toward them.

Rachel stuck her head out of the wagon. She held Davy nestled in her arms and Susanna snuggled up close.

Katie sighed. They all needed to be told. Together, maybe they could think of something.

"The cows went dry." Katie spoke at the same time Jason said. "I didn't get any milk tonight."

Tommy frowned. "Davy has to have milk. God has promised to supply all of our needs if we trust Him. Let's join hands and pray. Move over here by the wagon so Rachel can pray with us."

Jason and Tommy took Katie's hands before reaching up into the wagon to accept Rachel's. When Jason and Rachel completed the circle, they all bowed their heads, and Tommy led their prayer. "Lord, You know our need and will answer even before we pray. We believe you now to give us direction. Show us where to turn to find milk for Davy."

Katie added her silent prayers to the others and she felt better. God had heard them, and He would answer. Davy still didn't have milk for supper, but she refused to give in to worry. She returned to her soup and biscuits while the conversation centered on trying to coax more milk from the cows.

Katie turned toward the others. "If we only had one more cow that had milk, we'd be all right."

"Well, we don't have one more cow." Tommy's voice held a note of impatience. He walked away and stood with his head bowed, then swung toward Katie as a smile crept over his face. "You are right. We don't have another cow, but we do have Nanny."

"Nanny?" Katie shook her head. "We don't have Nanny anymore. Dad gave that goat to the Barletts a long time ago."

Tommy stood. "I'm going to go see them. My guess is they'll loan her to us once they hear of our need."

"Will she have milk?" Rachel asked. "I mean since the cows have quit maybe she has, too."

Tommy shook his head. "No, she isn't as likely to. Anyway, I'm going to see."

Jason stood. "I'll go with you, then I'd better get on back to camp. Ma Taylor would have my hide if I missed supper."

"You are coming back for Bible reading, aren't you?" As soon as the words were out, Katie wished she could call them back. It sounded like she didn't want Jason to leave. And she for sure didn't want him getting that idea.

He grinned at her. "Yeah, I'll be back. I wouldn't miss our Bible study. Save me a place to sit?"

She nodded as warmth covered her face. With a smile playing at the corners of her lips, she turned back to her cooking.

Before long Rachel joined her. "Is there something I can do? Davy is asleep, and Suzy is putting her baby doll to bed."

Katie laughed. "Ever since Davy's birth, Suzy has become a very good mother. She made Jason play with her dolly the other day. I was so surprised when he did." She turned away. "If you can find something to dish these beans on, I'd appreciate it. They—I mean—Tommy should be back by the time they're ready."

Rachel laughed. "You know he likes you, too."

"Tommy?"

"No, silly, the one who has you blushing every time he looks at you. Jason Barnett, of course."

Katie couldn't stop the flush from again warming her cheeks. "I don't—" She sighed. "All right, I am attracted to Jason, but I doubt he sees me as any more than Tommy's sister. Or worse, yet, he feels some sort of debt because of what happened to Karl."

Rachel frowned and looked across their camp before shaking her head. "No, I don't think Jason is blaming himself for Karl's death, not even a part of it. I've watched the two of you together, and I believe God has brought you to each other for a purpose. You belong together. Don't tell me you haven't thought the same thing."

Katie shook her head as tears stung her eyes. She blinked to hide them. "I won't, but why am I talking about it at all? If you must know, I'm in love with Jason. I've never met a more gentle, kind, compassionate man. He's the only man I ever felt the desire to spend my life with. Time is nothing when I'm with him. Honestly, Rachel, I could sit and visit with Jason forever. Oh, forget visiting. I could be with him forever without a word spoken and never grow tired."

Rachel smiled and hugged Katie. "You are in love with him. I knew it! Please, may I help you plan your wedding?"

Katie laughed and swiped at her eyes. "Oh, Rachel! Now look what you've done. Got me crying about a wedding that will never take place."

"Oh, it will take place." Rachel grinned as she turned to get some plates. "I think we can count on that."

"What of you and Tommy?" Katie called to her.

Rachel turned back around with wide eyes and no trace of humor on her face. "We weren't talking about me."

"Maybe we should."

"No, I don't think so. Tommy is a wonderful man, but he has no romantic interest in me. We're friends. That's all."

"You expect me to believe you have no romantic interest in Tommy?" Katie made a clicking noise with her tongue. "Christians do not tell lies, Rachel."

"Who says I have to tell you anything?" The hint of a smile touched Rachel's expression.

Katie stuck out her lower lip and tried to look hurt. "After I exposed my innermost feelings to you? Come on. I'm only asking because I care. I want Tommy to love you."

"All right." Rachel retraced her steps until she stood by Katie. "I love Tommy. There is not a question in my mind. He's everything I've ever wanted in a life mate. He's a wonderful Christian. He's caring and gentle. And he's handsome."

"Handsome?"

She laughed at Katie's raised eyebrows. "I think he's very handsome and that's what matters. You just can't see it because you're his sister."

Katie acted like she was thinking and then nodded. "Yes, you are probably right. At least I know he isn't overly ugly."

Both girls turned at a sound to the side. Tommy stepped from evening's dusk into their campfire's light. "I did it." A huge smile relaxed his face, and Katie had to agree with Rachel. Tommy was quite good looking, even if he was her brother.

"Mr. Barnett said they would gladly give us all the milk we need. He said Nanny is producing plenty. Mrs. Barnett said goat's milk is easier to digest, anyway, so Davy shouldn't have any trouble adjusting to it. We don't even have to milk her. Their oldest son is going to keep doing it."

"Praise God." Katie breathed a prayer of thanksgiving as her legs gave out and she plopped into the rocker. Davy would be all right.

~*~

Tommy sat in the gray autumn dusk on a wooden barrel near the fire where the light shone brightest for reading. He picked up his mother's Bible. "I'll be reading from the fourth chapter of John tonight."

At the fourteenth verse, he read, "But whosoever drinketh of the water that I shall give him shall never thirst; but the water that I shall give him shall be in him a well of water springing up into everlasting life."

Katie adjusted Davy's blanket around the bottle of goat's milk Isaac Bartlett had brought over earlier. His sucking made little slurping sounds that brought a smile to her face. She glanced to the side and caught Jason watching them. If only she could read his mind. He never failed to sit beside her when they had the Bible readings. Probably so he could hold Susanna, but Suzy was with Rachel tonight. She shook her head to drive away the questions that realization brought. She needed to concentrate on what Tommy said.

"Every one of us knows what it's like to be thirsty. Many times in the last few months I've sucked on a smooth, hard pebble just to keep from feeling the thirst that our trek across the desert caused. I know you did the same. But Jesus isn't talking about a physical thirst. How many of us have felt that intense longing deep within that only Jesus can satisfy? I have, not so long ago."

Katie looked to the side where Clay stood again on the outskirts of those gathered around the campfire. Many had brought quilts or warm, woolen blankets for a shield from the cool air sweeping out of the north as a gentle reminder that winter would soon be upon them.

Small children snuggled into their parent's laps and many were already asleep. The adults listened as Tommy spoke. Katie glanced again at Clay. He appeared to be listening as well. She closed her eyes for a moment and breathed a prayer for his salvation.

"And now I'd like for her to come forward to give her testimony." Tommy's voice rang out catching Katie's attention.

Everyone turned to look at her. She must have missed hearing something important.

Jason nudged her with his elbow. "Go on. Tommy wants you to tell about your salvation."

She looked from him to Davy. He reached for the baby. "Let me hold him."

Her eyes widened. He would hold a baby in public? "You want to hold Davy?"

He grinned. "Sure. He hasn't gotten that heavy, has he?"

She shook her head in amazement and handed him over. "Just keep the bottle in his mouth, and you should be fine. Rachel's right over there with Suzy if you need help."

"Go on. We'll be fine."

Katie stepped around people until she stood beside Tommy. All she could think of was that from this view point the crowd seemed to have doubled. Her gaze skimmed over so many and focused on the Parkers. They were here? *Please Lord, don't let me say anything to offend them.* Her voice shook as she said, "I don't really know how to do this, but I can tell you about the night I turned from my rebellion to accept what God offered."

She glanced at Tommy and he nodded his encouragement so she began. "I guess if my mother was here, she would say I was her rebellious child. I liked to do things my way. She didn't approve of dancing, but I went to every dance I could. Having fun was most important to me."

Her gaze met Clay's and stopped. Her talk might influence someone's life. Even his. Or the Parkers. Maybe several were in need of salvation. She breathed a quick prayer for help, and her gaze settled on Jason. He sent encouragement in his smile. She would tell her story to him and Rachel, the Bartletts and the Taylors. She could talk to them while the others listened. She could do this.

"My Christian mother is now enjoying the blessings of her heavenly home. I wish I had listened to her from the start, but I rebelled against her teachings.

"When we started on this journey, I was angry at my father for making us come. I turned my anger toward God when my little brother died in the first river we crossed. I became bitter, and I hurt so bad inside. Then Tommy started whistling and singing hymns and reading the Bible. He changed so much I knew something real had happened to him. I saw the difference, and I watched him. He had truly changed. Before long, his life convinced me that I wanted whatever he had."

She glanced at Tommy, and he gave her an encouraging nod. "Then my dad was killed. I couldn't tell him I was sorry for blaming him for all that was wrong in my life and for being angry at him. That's when I realized my rebellion was not his fault. The anger at him and at God was my problem, not his. But I couldn't tell him then because he was gone, and that hurt so bad. I became so miserable I went to my mother. She was waiting for me with this Bible."

Katie lifted the Bible from Tommy's hands. She felt a stirring of love and concern for others as she glanced around the circle of friends and fellow travelers.

"That night Mama talked and prayed with me. I told God how sorry I was for all my resentment and anger. I accepted

Jesus Christ as my savior, and I'm so glad I did. This terribly hard trail we're traveling didn't get any easier. As a matter of fact, it got a lot harder when Mama died. But now I have a source of strength and help I never had before. God's Spirit goes with me, guiding me and comforting me. I'm still growing and learning, but my life has been changed, and if yours hasn't been, it can be tonight."

Katie handed the Bible back to Tommy and returned to Jason's side. She reached for Davy, but he shook his head. "No, he's fine."

"Jason, give my baby back to me." She whispered.

He just grinned and pulled Davy further away, then inclined his head toward Tommy who was talking again. Katie glared at him before turning her attention to her brother. He'd get tired of holding Davy soon enough. No need to make a scene.

Tommy's exhortation of the fourth chapter of Saint John didn't last long, but surely the Word had not fallen on deaf ears. When he asked if any would like to accept Jesus as their Savior, a young couple stepped forward.

Katie forgot her tiff with Jason, as she thrilled that Tommy's efforts were bearing fruit. She watched when Tommy called Rachel to his side to help pray with the woman. Rachel hesitated just a moment before slipping out from under Susanna who had fallen asleep on her lap. She joined Tommy and together they prayed with the young couple. Katie brushed moisture from her eyes. They made a wonderful team working together for the Lord. Why couldn't her brother see it?

Then, Katie's breath caught in her throat when she noticed the Parkers standing in front of Tommy. They knelt together as Mr. Bartlett and Mr. Taylor both joined them.

Lord, be with them. Tears filled Katie's eyes. God surely answered prayers. She laid her hand on her baby's blanket, so thankful to have him. Jason looked up and raised his eyebrows. Davy slept and needed to be in his crib. Katie leaned closer to whisper. "Let me take him and put him to bed." She reached for him and this time Jason didn't object.

As she walked toward the wagon, Jason joined the others

who were still praying. Katie settled Davy in his crib and then unable to stay away from the activity outside, climbed down from the wagon. Clay stepped out of the shadows, and she jumped. "Oh, I didn't know anyone was here."

"I'm sorry. I didn't mean to scare you." He stood with his hands in his pockets. A frown creased his forehead.

Katie smiled. "It's all right. I'm glad you've been coming to our Bible studies."

"I've enjoyed them—more than I thought I would—and I've learned a lot. Your talk was real nice." Clay seemed nervous and kept looking toward those praying.

"Thank you."

Clay turned back. "Uh, Katie." He hesitated and then rushed on. "I owe you an apology. I made a mess of things. I know you've changed. Well, I have, too. When Mary Beth got burned so bad, it did something to me. She'll get ok, I guess, but she'll always be scarred. I've been fighting a battle since the night it happened when I thought she might die. That's why I'm here now. I've got to talk to Tommy. I know what you all have is real. It's what I need."

Katie's heart leapt for joy. She started to say how glad she was, but he turned away.

He took a step toward Tommy then turned back. "Maybe after I talk to him, we can have us a talk. Do you think so?"

She nodded and watched him walk away. Her excitement of the evening faded. Clay had not rejected her. He'd been burdened in his soul and could think of nothing else. Was this God's leading? She'd been praying for God's direction in her life. The burden of caring for Susanna and Davy was not a light one. Someday she expected to marry, and she wanted God's choice in her husband. Maybe Clay was the right one. Her mind whirled with the possibilities. She needed to be alone to think and pray.

She climbed back into the wagon and lay on her mattress while she compared the two men, Clay and Jason. She liked Clay. Actually, she liked him very much. She had enjoyed the few times he'd kissed her. Jason had never done more than hold her hand. Did she love Clay? She searched her heart and came away empty. Did she love Jason? There was no need to search her heart for that answer. Yes, she loved Jason.

The problem was not in her, but in the two men. Clay had declared his love for her and told her he planned to make her his wife. Yet the man she loved had done little more than befriend her. Just as she told Rachel, he treated her as Tommy's little sister. Even tonight, he had sat beside her so he could hold Davy. Always with him it was the children. Why not her?

"Lord, please direct my paths. If Clay is the one You have chosen, I ask for love to fill my heart for him. If You see Your way clear to choose Jason for my husband, please place a love for me within his heart. Amen."

Katie went to sleep thinking of Jason, remembering each time she'd spent with him, trying to find some proof he loved her. When she woke early the next morning Jason came first to her mind. Come what may, she would confront him before they reached Oregon. If Jason could not declare his love for her, she would marry Clay. Surely, it was better to marry a man who loved her than to marry a man she loved, but who could not return that love.

Chapter 17

*K*atie climbed out of the wagon after putting Susanna and Davy down for the night. Tommy's and Jason's muffled voices had kept her on edge for the last few minutes. She stepped around to the side where they were kneeling beside the back wheel. "What are you doing?"

"Checking the axles." Tommy answered without looking up.

Katie's eyes connected with Jason's.

He grinned. "The grease packed in the axle keeps the wheel turning smoothly. We're getting into the Blue Mountains now, and the climb is hard on the wagons."

"Ah, the breakdowns I've been hearing about the last couple of days." She took a step back.

He nodded. "Right. Tommy wants to be sure your wagon's going to make it."

"I see." Katie turned away and almost ran into someone. "Oh, excuse me."

"You're fine, Katie." Clay caught her elbow then pulled his hand away. "Hello, Tommy. Jason."

"Evening, Clay." Tommy glanced up. "Got your wagon in good shape for the climb?"

"Sure do." Clay nodded. "My dad and I just finished doing the same thing you're doing. Thought I'd stop by and see Katie for a minute."

Tommy made an unintelligible grunt, and Jason seemed especially interested in the wheel Tommy was working on.

Katie walked away from them, and Clay followed. She'd rather keep things quiet around the wagon where the kids were sleeping. Not that she expected Susanna to wake easily, but Davy might. Several feet from the wagon she stopped.

Jason appeared to be watching. He turned away. Maybe he hadn't been. She felt like stomping her foot. Why couldn't he show some signs of jealousy? She looked at Clay. "I'd offer you a chair, but we only have one rocker."

He shrugged. "I don't mind. Did Tommy tell you what happened to me last night?"

Katie nodded. "Yes, and I'm so glad you have become a Christian, Clay. I couldn't be happier for you. I know what a difference it makes."

"Yes, I'm beginning to find out." He glanced at the other men. "Could we go for a walk like we used to?"

Katie laughed. "I didn't have a baby back then, Clay."

"A baby?" Clay's eyes grew wide before a frown settled on his handsome face.

"Yes, a baby. Remember my little brother?"

"Oh." He glanced around. "Can't Tommy watch him?"

Katie shook her head. "Tommy is busy. Rachel is gone with her mother for the moment, and Davy is sleeping in the wagon so I can't take him with me."

"What about your little sister?"

"Suzy is five years old, Clay. She isn't old enough to take care of a baby, even a sleeping baby."

"In that case, I guess we'll have to stay here and talk."

Katie nodded. "Yes, I guess so."

Clay didn't stay long, and Katie was glad. When she wouldn't go walking with him, he didn't say anything of importance. Would he have if they'd been out of Tommy's and Jason's hearing range? She watched him walk into the darkness and wondered. If he should propose again, would she be making a mistake by accepting? She'd forgotten how tiring he could become after a few minutes of useless talking. *Thank you, Lord, that he didn't propose.*

Maybe she'd be better off remaining single. How could she raise two children without a husband's help? Tommy would do what he could. Then, he'd marry Rachel and where would she be? She couldn't live with them, and she couldn't bear the thought of turning Davy over to anyone else, not even Rachel.

She sighed and turned to her mother's rocking chair. From

the looks of things, she didn't have a choice. Surely, there were a lot worse things than marriage to Clay. She could do it. She was no longer the selfish, young girl she had been five months ago. After suffering through thirst and hunger, worn and soiled clothing, and no way to clean either it or herself, she'd learned to accept the bad along with the good. She had the Lord to lean on. If Clay was God's plan for her and the children, she would gladly marry him.

Yet a thorn pricked at her soul. That thorn was her love for Jason. She bowed her head. *Lord God, if it be your will, please removed my love for Jason so I may learn to love Clay. Not my will, but Thine be done.*

~*~

"Oh, Katie, look ahead." Rachel pointed toward what appeared to be an oasis in the midst of the rugged mountains they had been in for days.

"Is it possible to see a mirage in the mountains?" Katie's eyes feasted on the beautiful green valley before them.

Rachel laughed. "No, I think that's just in the desert. This must be for real. Don't you think it's time we had a place to rest our spirits? God is so good to provide rest just when we feel we can't take another step."

"Yes, and I'm ready for it." Katie's pace picked up, and Davy swung back and forth in the special sling hanging from her shoulders. She had fashioned it for him from the material of one of their mother's dresses when he became too heavy to carry comfortably.

The motion of the sling excited Davy into flinging his arms and kicking his legs. Rachel laughed at his antics. "You'd better slow down, or he's going to kick his way out of there."

Katie laughed as she slowed. She took Davy from the sling and nuzzled his soft baby neck. His mouth spread into a big grin, and he chortled his baby delight. "You precious little doll. You and Suzy are the two bright spots in this whole terrible experience."

At the sound of her name, Susanna looked up at her sister. "I'm a bright spot of what?"

Katie laughed with Rachel before answering. "You are a

bright spot of sunshine, little sister. That means I love you very much."

Susanna grinned. "I love you, too, Katie. And I love Rachel. And Tommy. And Jason. And I love Rachel's Ma and Pa Morgan, too."

"Well, you're just full of love today, aren't you?" Katie slipped Davy back into the sling after one more kiss.

Rachel looked from Davy to Katie. "What are you going to teach him to call you?"

Katie looked up startled. "I—I don't know. Katie, I guess." She stammered. "I don't actually feel like his sister, but I'm really not his mother, either. Maybe I should just let him decide on his own. I hadn't thought."

"What about Jason?"

Rachel's voice was so soft Katie thought she'd misunderstood until she looked into her friend's eyes and saw the concern. Still, she pretended she didn't understand.

"I suppose he'll call him Jason. Or Mr. Barnett."

"That isn't what I meant." A smile curved Rachel's mouth. "What would happen if you got Jason away from everyone where he'd have to listen to you and where you could force the issue of your love?"

Katie gasped. "Rachel, what are you talking about? I can't force any issue with Jason or any man. If he loved me, he'd let me know."

Rachel sighed. "I suppose, but I wonder if he knows how you feel. Maybe he's afraid of you. Men have insecurities the same as we do. I'm sure of it. Unless they're so full of themselves they can't imagine a woman turning them down. Jason isn't like that."

"So you think I should talk to him?" How many times had she thought the same thing? Was this the answer to her prayers? Oh, she hoped so. Katie's heart pounded.

Rachel nodded. "Yes, I think you should try to talk to him if you can. Pray about it and see if the opportunity presents itself. Maybe it will while we're camped here in the valley."

"If Mr. Colton calls a rest." The air continued to grow colder as each week passed. They couldn't afford to take too many stops before they reached Oregon City. Now, so near the end of their journey, everyone sensed the need to hurry. Katie met Rachel's searching eyes with a smile. "All right. I'll continue to pray about this and see what happens."

"I want to know what he says." Rachel laughed. "I'm excited for you."

~*~

As Katie had hoped, Mr. Colton called a halt for the night in the middle of the valley where the animals would have plenty of grass. Katie's heart thumped out her insecurities and fear as the thought of confronting Jason nagged at her.

She hurried through supper, keeping constant watch for Jason to stroll into their camp. Tommy left for a while, and she was alone with the children. Susanna seemed to be dawdling more than usual.

"Hurry and eat, Suzy. I want to get the dishes washed and put away." She gathered hers and Tommy's and set them to the side.

"I am hurrying, Katie." Susanna flashed an annoyed look toward her then licked her empty spoon.

Katie sighed. "Maybe if you put something on your spoon, you could eat faster."

Susanna stuck her face up toward Katie and made exaggerated chewing motions. "I have to chew. Mama said so."

At the mention of Mama, Katie's heart constricted. If only Mama were here now. And Dad. She'd still be a carefree young girl planning for her next dance. But was that what she wanted to do with her life? Act like a spoiled child who gave little thought for anyone except herself? She hadn't asked for the responsibility of raising two small children, but she didn't resent them either. She sighed and turned away to wash the dishes. Let Suzy chew all she wanted. Her plate could be washed later.

"Katie, I hope I'm not intruding."

Katie swung toward the woman's voice and found Rachel's mother standing a few feet away. "No, of course not. How are you tonight?"

"Oh, I'm fine." Mrs. Morgan smiled. "I have a favor to ask.

153

I wondered if you'd let Suzy come over to our camp for a little bit. We found a turtle and thought she might like to see it. I could bring it over here, but we'd love to enjoy her company if you don't mind."

Katie turned toward Suzy who still sat playing with her food. "I don't mind at all if you're sure you want her. I'd like for her to finish eating first though. So far she's been more interested in playing."

Mrs. Morgan laughed. "From what I've seen, that's normal behavior at her age. Do you mind if I speak to her? Maybe the promise of a turtle will help her eat faster."

"Anything you can do would be wonderful." Katie watched Mrs. Morgan lean close to Susanna and speak to her. She couldn't hear every word, but Susanna brightened at the word turtle and stuffed a spoonful of beans into her mouth. Katie laughed. Maybe she should catch a turtle and keep it as a pet. No, the new would soon wear off, and her sister would go back to her old ways.

Susanna ran over with her plate and silverware as Katie finished everything else. "Here, Katie. I'm all done. Can I go with Rachel's Ma to visit?"

"Yes, you may. Thank you for eating." Katie slipped the plate in the water. "Thank you, Mrs. Morgan. Tommy or I one will be here when she wears out her welcome."

With a laugh, Mrs. Morgan waved Katie's words aside. "I doubt that could happen. Suzy's such a sweet, little girl. I'll bring her back before bedtime, though."

Katie checked on Davy in his makeshift cradle. He was playing contentedly with his hands. She watched his tiny brow furrow as he concentrated on the wiggling fingers before his eyes. He was so adorable. Would he eventually develop that streak of rebellion she already recognized in Susanna? The same desire to rebel she had before she gave it all up to the Lord. She hoped not.

"He's all right, isn't he?"

Katie swung around, her hand over her heart. "Tommy Donovan, don't sneak up on me like that."

He laughed. "Sorry, I figured you heard me."

"Well, I didn't." She glanced past him and saw no one.

"Jason isn't coming over tonight. He's helping Mr. Taylor with some repairs on their wagon."

Katie turned back to Davy to hide her face from her brother. "I don't know why you're telling me what Jason's doing. I was just thinking about taking Davy for a walk before bedtime. He's wide awake now."

"Fine, I've got some studying to do." Tommy looked around. "Where's Suzy?"

Katie grinned. "Oh, it is quieter than usual around here, isn't it?"

Tommy lifted his eyebrows. "What did you do, put her to bed early?"

"Oh course not." Katie tried to act offended. "It just so happens she's visiting the Morgans. Rachel's mother came to get her because they found a turtle for her to play with. Can you imagine? She said she'd bring her back before bedtime."

"Okay." Tommy shrugged. "I'll be here. I want to do some studying before Bible study tomorrow night."

Katie watched her brother get his Bible from the wagon and marveled at the change in him. When he settled in the rocking chair, she stepped closer. "Tommy, is God calling you to preach?"

His eyes widened as they connected with hers. When he swallowed, his Adam's apple bobbed. "Actually, I think He may be. Why'd you ask?"

"Because that's exactly what you have been doing. You've had some wonderful successes, too. Look at Clay not to mention the others. How about the Parkers? Did they accept Christ? I never heard."

He smiled. "Yes, both of them did that night."

"That's wonderful."

"I know. I'm grateful God is using me this way. And you. I think it was your testimony that got to them."

Katie shook her head. God could have used her testimony, but it was Tommy who drew the people with his commentary on the scriptures and his easy way with people. "You know, Tommy, you're going to need a wife. I thought you and Rachel made a wonderful team the other night when you prayed together for that first couple."

Tommy frowned. "I need to make that decision on my own, don't you think?"

Katie felt the rebuke. "I suppose. Along with Rachel."

"Yeah." He grinned. "Or someone else."

"Tommy!" Katie raised her voice. "There isn't anyone else, is there?"

Tommy gave her a piercing look. "No, there isn't. But it's still my decision."

"All right." Katie decided she needed to mind her own business even though she believed he was making a mistake. A tiny cry sounded from the cradle. "I'll be back later. Davy probably needs a diaper change then we're going for a walk."

"Suit yourself." Tommy opened his Bible.

Katie changed Davy then lifted him, tucking the blanket securely around his flailing arms and legs. He seemed to know they were going to do something special as his mouth spread wide in a big grin.

She didn't even make it away from their camp when Clay stepped out of the shadows. "Katie, I'd like to talk to you."

"All right." Inwardly, she sighed. Her talk with Jason would have to keep.

He looked at Davy. "I see you're watching your brother again tonight."

"Watching my brother?" Katie frowned, trying to understand him. "Why do you call it that? I always watch him because I'm the only mother he has."

"The only mother?" Now Clay frowned.

"Yes, Clay. My mother died leaving him in my care. You know that. She asked me to raise him as my own son." She took a deep breath and let it out slowly. "Let's go over here." Katie pulled a wooden box far enough from Tommy to give them privacy and sat down with Davy cuddled close.

When he didn't speak, she decided she might as well try to find out what he wanted. She didn't care how forward it might sound. "You asked me to marry you once. You said you would win my heart before we reached Oregon. We're almost there now. Do you still want to marry me?"

Clay sat on an overturned barrel. He looked at his hands as he twisted them between his knees. The silence seemed to stretch on forever before he looked up and met her gaze. "I didn't plan on a ready-made family, Katie."

"I didn't either, Clay. But I have one now. Suzy may choose to go with me, too. But Davy doesn't have a choice. He is mine."

Clay shook his head. "You know, Katie, I don't think I've won your heart, have I?"

Now it was Katie's turn to look away. She didn't want him to see the turmoil in her eyes. Finally, she turned back to him. "As a Christian, I can't lie to you. No, Clay, I've lost my heart, but not to you. I'm sorry."

He shook his head. "No, don't be. I guess I was never really in love with you, anyway. I think more than anything you were a challenge to me. You seemed so wild and free. I wanted to tame you. But the trail did that, didn't it?"

Katie nodded. "Yes, it did. I've suffered a lot of heartache, but you know what that's like. You've been tamed, too, Clay. When we turned our lives over to God, he remade us in His image. Now we need to study His Word and pray so we can conform to that image. I think that's the true taming, don't you?"

"Yeah, I'm sure it is. Katie, a while ago you said you had lost your heart to someone else. It's Jason Barnett, isn't it?"

Katie laughed. "Is it that easy to see through me?"

Clay's cocky grin settled into place. "Only when you look at him."

Katie shook her head. "I'm sorry, Clay. Things don't always turn out the way we plan them, do they?"

"No, but you know I do love you, Katie."

He grinned at her surprised look. "You're my sister in Christ now, and I'll always love you as a brother should. I hope you feel the same way about me."

Katie smiled. "I do, Clay, and I always will. Thank you for understanding."

She stood and took a step toward him. He stood, too, and

smiled down at her. On impulse, Katie shifted Davy into one arm then reached up and pulled Clay down so she could kiss his cheek. She was surprised when he gave her a hug and squeezed, holding her for just a moment.

He stepped back then. "I'll see you around, Katie. I wish you the best with Jason. If he's got half a brain in his head, he won't let you get away."

Katie grinned. "I hope he's got at least half a brain, then."

Clay laughed and walked away with a wave, Katie saw movement to the side. When she looked, she saw Jason turn and fade into the shadows. Her heart lurched.

Tommy called to her. "What was that all about?"

She swung toward him. "Tommy, was Jason here?"

Her brother's eyebrows shot up. "No, Clay was. What did he want?"

"Clay and I had a nice talk and from the looks of things I'm going to grow up to be an old maid." Katie tried to make light of her situation.

Tommy turned and stood as Mr. and Mrs. Parker stepped into their light. Katie pulled Davy close and faced them. Had they heard her? They could say a woman alone had no business raising a baby when he could have a loving mother and father.

Mr. Parker nodded at Tommy. "Good evening."

"Evening, Mr. Parker." Tommy offered his hand and the two men shook.

The older man looked from one to the other. "I don't suppose you're happy to see us, and I can't really blame you. We've come to apologize for the way we acted before."

"You mean you don't want Davy now?" The words left Katie's mouth before she could stop them.

"Oh, no." Mrs. Parker spoke. "We'd take him in a minute, if you'd change your minds about giving him up."

"We haven't." This came from Tommy.

"That's what we figured." Mr. Parker said. "We've watched you, and we can't find any fault unless it's that you hold him too much. You can spoil a baby that way, you know."

"At least he knows we love him." Katie felt a glimmer of hope at their words. Were they backing away?

Mrs. Parker looked at Katie. "Are you sure it isn't too much for you? Caring for a baby is a big responsibility, and you already have a little girl to take care of."

Katie smiled. How well she knew the responsibility of caring for two small children. "With Rachel and me working together, Davy and Suzy are not too much."

Mrs. Parker smiled then. "I can see you love him very much. We won't bother you again. Please, may I hold him for just a minute before we go?"

Katie reluctantly handed the baby to her and watched as she gently pulled the blanket back. Davy's little hand reached out and touched her face. Mrs. Parker bent and kissed his forehead before handing him back to Katie. Unshed tears stood in her eyes. "If he was mine, I couldn't give him up either. I don't blame you."

She turned to her husband. "Let's go back to our wagon and leave these kids alone."

Mr. Parker nodded. "We'll be at Bible study tomorrow night. I sure appreciate what you kids are doing."

As soon as they left, Katie turned to Tommy. "Do you think they'll be back?"

Tommy shook his head. "No, I think we've seen the last of them as far as Davy's concerned. God worked in their lives the other night."

Katie nodded. "I think you're right." She sighed. "I was taking Davy for a walk, but I feel exhausted all of a sudden. I think I'll turn in instead."

As she put Davy in his little cradle, she glanced to where she thought she'd seen Jason. Had he listened to her and Clay? If so, he knew they'd agreed to be only friends. Why hadn't he stayed? Or had she only imagined she saw him? If only she could confront him as she had Clay. If she did, would the outcome be the same? Her heart sank at the thought. She couldn't be only friends with Jason.

Chapter 18

*G*rande Ronde. The name was as beautiful as the valley. Katie looked around the lush, green valley stretching for twenty miles through the Blue Mountains. The early months on the trail seemed forever ago. Would they ever reach Oregon and the end of their journey? Not only did the trail seem to go on forever, but they were running out of food.

The trail through the Blue Mountains had been rougher than any they had traveled before. The weather grew colder almost daily with the nights long and dark. Tommy had butchered all the cows he could spare and now even that meat was practically gone. Jason no longer rode herd on their cows full time since those with cattle had decided to combine the few remaining animals together and take turns driving them. Katie shivered at the thought of what might become of them if they didn't get more to eat.

She longed to talk to Jason, but he seemed to be avoiding her. He hadn't spoken to her since the night Clay stopped by and they agreed to be friends. He still came to Tommy's Bible study, but they only met once a week now. Jason always found a place to sit on the opposite side away from her on those nights. Not even the thought of holding Davy or Susanna enticed him to come near her. Several times Katie had tried to approach him, but he always managed to slip away before she could get his attention. Finally, in desperation, she went to Tommy.

"Do you know what's wrong with Jason?"

Tommy looked up from the wheel he had been checking. "Nothing that I know of. Why?"

"He won't come near me anymore."

Tommy shrugged. "He acts the same to me."

"Then, why don't you talk to him? Find out what's wrong."

"Katie, no." Tommy sat back on his heels and shook his head. "If you mean for me to ask him how he feels about you, I can't do that."

"Why not?" Desperation drove Katie. "I haven't done anything to him. If he's mad at me for any reason, don't you think he should tell me about it?"

Tommy looked past Katie and shrugged. "Probably. Here he comes now. Why don't you ask him yourself?"

Katie twirled around with her heart beating double time. She saw Jason heading their way as if he were on a mission. He stopped a few feet from her and nodded before turning his attention to Tommy.

"How are you folks doing for meat?"

Tommy gave a short laugh. "I'd say we're about out."

"So are we. How would you like to go hunting?"

Tommy stood and looked across the valley toward the forest near the foot of the mountains. "Might be a good idea while we have the time."

Katie glared at Jason. He'd scarcely looked at her when he walked up and now stood with his back half turned toward her as if she were invisible. She had done nothing to deserve this treatment. If Jason wanted nothing to do with her, the least he could do was tell her so to her face. Surely, he wasn't so dense he didn't know she cared for him.

"How soon will it take you to get ready to go?" Jason stood with his arms crossed facing Tommy.

If she stomped his foot, maybe he would notice her then. Her toes twitched, daring her to do so. Then she stopped as an idea took root in her mind. A hunting trip? Into the mountains away from everyone else except Jason? What a wonderful idea. If she tagged along, Jason would have to talk to her. Rachel would go, too, if she asked, to keep Tommy occupied while she found out what was wrong with Jason. She was sure of it.

"I want to go along."

Jason swung around at her voice. Tommy's eyes widened. Both men stared at her as if she'd sprouted a second head.

Tommy shook his head. "You can't go, Katie."

"Yes, I can." A spark of Katie's old reckless spirit returned as she challenged Tommy. "Mrs. Morgan has wanted to take care of Suzy ever since she kept her the night Davy was born. When she took her over to see that turtle, she said they had a wonderful time. She offered to watch her again anytime. I know she'd love to watch Davy, too, so Rachel can go with us. It'll be an outing we all deserve."

Jason stared at her.

Tommy shook his head. "Tramping through the woods looking for animals to kill is not an outing. It's no job for women. Why don't you stay here where you belong and take care of the youngsters. You could get hurt out there."

Katie felt the heat of battle rising. "Where I belong? None of us belong on this treacherous trail, Tommy, but we're here, anyway. I could get hurt right here at the wagon. Others have. You could get hurt out there in the woods, Tommy Donovan. Jason could get hurt. You can't stop us. Rachel and I are going if we have to follow you."

"Where are we going?" Rachel stepped up beside Katie. "I heard my name as I came over."

Katie swung around to her friend. "We're going hunting with Tommy and Jason. Do you think your mother would like to watch Susanna and Davy for a while?"

Rachel smiled. "She'd love to."

"See." Katie swung back to Tommy. "Rachel wants to go, too."

Tommy glanced toward Jason as if seeking his support.

Jason shrugged. "I suppose we could take care of them."

Katie let out a very unladylike snort. As if they needed taken care of like some simpering female from back east. She opened her mouth to object, then shut it. If she wanted to go, she probably shouldn't challenge his less than complimentary opinion of her and Rachel. She waited to see what Tommy's decision would be.

He glared at her while her heart tried to pound its way out of her chest. She refused to back down and made sure her gaze didn't flicker.

He looked away first and took a deep breath before letting

it out in a rush. "I guess you can go, but don't blame me if one of you gets hurt."

Katie shared a jubilant smile with Rachel.

~*~

Fifteen minutes later, Katie tromped beside Rachel behind Tommy and Jason through waist high grass toward the forest-covered mountains. They entered a dense forest of Douglas fir, pines, cedars, and redwood. As they went farther into the woods, Katie could hear the rustling of small animals scurrying out of their way. She glanced at Rachel who motioned for her to keep quiet.

Katie nodded. They were too close to camp for her to mess up now and get sent back. Tommy was itching to find a reason to do just that. Jason probably was, too.

Tommy's rifle rested on his shoulder. He stopped and held up one hand in warning before he swung the rifle down and took aim.

Katie didn't see anything. She followed the direction his gun pointed, then she noticed a deer standing motionless no more than thirty yards from them. She held her breath. If he missed, it wouldn't be her fault.

Tommy's gun roared. The deer jumped and ran a few feet then fell over.

"Good shot." Jason complimented him. "Now if we could get another one or two we'd be set for a few days. At least for our families."

Tommy nodded. "We're not far from camp. Why don't I clean it and take it back? Katie can help me since she insisted on coming."

No! Katie wanted to scream at her brother. He knew she wanted to talk to Jason. Why would he do this? She sent a silent appeal to him with her eyes.

Rachel looked at Katie and stepped forward. "I'll help you. I'd like to go back, anyway."

"Why don't you girls both go with Tommy?" Jason looked everywhere except at Katie as if he was afraid of her. "I can manage on my own."

"Jason." Katie waited until he looked at her. Then she

spoke in a soft, firm voice. "I'm staying."

"I don't think that's such a good idea, Katie." Jason met her challenge with one of his own.

"I think it is." She lifted her chin in a stubborn gesture. "I'm tired of being ignored, Jason. I want some answers."

"In that case, I think Rachel and I should be heading back." Tommy ran the short distance to his deer as if eager to get away from them.

Rachel gave Katie an encouraging smile before following Tommy.

Jason stood frowning at Tommy for several heartbeats before he turned his frown on Katie and grabbed her elbow. "Fine, then come on."

He pulled her away from Tommy and Rachel deeper into the woods. She stumbled through the forest floor of dried leaves and twigs until he finally stopped. She could still see Tommy and Rachel, but they would have a hard time overhearing whatever Jason had to say. Katie's heart raced and her knees wobbled from fear. What had she done? Jason was obviously angry with her. A man who cared wouldn't act like this. She glanced the direction they'd come into the forest. Why hadn't she stayed at camp? She'd made such a mess of everything.

Jason released her elbow and stepped back. He folded his arms and glared at her. "What was that all about?"

His belligerent stance stirred her anger, giving her the strength she needed to confront him. She folded her arms and lifted her chin. "What? Me staying?"

"You saying you're tired of being ignored."

Katie tossed her head. "Well, you should know."

Jason threw his hands out in a helpless gesture and shook his head. "I always heard women were impossible to understand. Now I believe it."

"Women are? You're the one who's been ignoring me."

"I'm not ignoring you." Jason's voice rose. "I'm looking at you. I'm talking to you. Where could you get the idea I'm ignoring you?"

"What you're doing is yelling at me." Katie's voice rose, too. When Tommy and Rachel straightened and stared at them, she lowered her voice. "But even this is better than pretending I don't exist."

She fought hurt and tears but refused to cry. Instead, she met Jason's frown with determination. "I've scarcely seen you since the night Tommy asked me to give my testimony. Since then, I don't think you've said more than two words to me."

Jason's frown deepened, and he looked away. "Yeah, well I didn't figure you wanted me bothering you."

"And you say women are hard to understand." Katie let out an exasperated sound with a rush of air as her hands flew out to the side. "Why on earth wouldn't I want you to talk to me?"

Jason kept his face averted. "I may not be the smartest guy around, but I know when I've lost."

"Lost what?" Katie shook her head. "I don't know what you're talking about, Jason."

His shoulders slumped as if all the fight had gone out of him. "Clay Monroe became a Christian the night you testified, didn't he?"

Katie nodded, totally confused. What did Clay have to do with this?

Jason turned and met her eyes. "He came to see you the next night. Remember? I was there helping Tommy with the wagon."

Again Katie nodded.

Jason averted his gaze. "I didn't get the message right then. A few nights later, I decided to come and see you." A harsh laugh escaped. "I saw plenty. When I got close to your wagon, I realized you already had company. You were sitting down holding Davy with Clay sitting close by. Then you both stood."

"I did see you. Why didn't you stay? I wanted to talk to you."

Jason's smile looked more like a grimace to Katie. "Stay for what? I left when I saw you kiss Clay, and he put his arms around you. Clay's a Christian now and so are you. There's no reason why you shouldn't have a wonderful life together."

As Jason talked, Katie's heart rejoiced, and she wanted to laugh and cry. Because, whether he knew it or not, Jason had just told her he loved her. Jason really did love her.

"Oh, Jason, I love you, too."

"I figured you loved him. Why else would you kiss him that way?" The misery on Jason's face warmed Katie's heart.

She couldn't hold back her laughter any longer. "Jason, I said I love *you*. Not Clay."

Jason's eyes lifted to search her face as if trying to unravel a puzzle.

Katie had never been happier. She laughed again. "I kissed him on the cheek because we had just agreed that our relationship as brother and sister in Christ was enough."

She giggled at Jason's confused expression. Boldness came to her from the truth she'd just learned. He loved her. He thought she wanted Clay so he stayed away. What would he do if she told him? She wavered, wanting to blurt everything out, but afraid of his rejection. Finally, her impulsive nature won. "He also wished me the best with you. He said if you had half a brain, you wouldn't let me get away."

Jason blinked then stared at Katie. "Clay doesn't want you?"

Katie laughed. "He didn't say that. He mostly said he hadn't planned on getting a ready-made family. And that he'd never really fallen in love with me, just as I hadn't him."

Jason made a sound that was unintelligible. "What about you, Katie? How do you feel about Clay?"

Katie smiled. "I don't want Clay. I already told you, I'm not in love with him if that's what you mean."

Jason grabbed Katie's shoulders and held her at arm's length as if the truth had finally penetrated his befuddled brain. He stared into her upturned face as if afraid to believe what she said. "Are you sure you're not in love with him? Or anyone else?"

Katie sighed. "Of course I'm in love with someone else, Jason. I've already told you. I'm in love with you."

"You love me?"

She nodded. Would he ever get it through his thick skull?

Jason shook his head. "I can't believe I've wasted all this time. The night I saw you kiss Clay—"

Katie tapped the side of her face. "On the cheek."

Jason grinned and repeated. "On the cheek. I was on my way to ask you a question."

"You were?" Katie's heart thudded. She knew what she wanted the question to be, but insecurity rose up inside and stole her confidence. Jason might never ask the question she wanted to hear. He hadn't said he loved her. She could be reading her own desires into his actions.

"Yes, I was. But after what I saw, I decided to go back to the Taylor's wagon and resign myself to living alone."

"You don't want to live alone for the rest of your life, do you, Jason?"

He released her and stepped back. He cupped a hand under his opposite elbow and stroked his chin. A glint came into his eyes as he drawled, "Well now, I don't know. Living alone has its merits."

"Jason!"

"Figure it out, Katie." Jason shrugged. "The man who gets you is going to have to take that baby boy and your little sister, too. It takes a special man to want a ready-made family like that."

The strength drained from Katie as she realized Jason might not be kidding. Clay hadn't wanted her brother and sister. Maybe Jason didn't either. She looked away to keep him from seeing the hurt in her eyes.

His hands closed over her arms as he turned her back toward him. "Look at me, Katie." His voice, no longer teasing, held a firm gentleness.

Katie turned to meet his gaze. Whatever he had to say, she could survive just as she had every other disappointment and hurt these last several months. Losing Jason wouldn't be as hard as losing her brother and her parents because he'd never belonged to her in the first place.

Jason slid his hands down her arms until his fingers closed around hers. He knelt in front of her, his serious gaze never leaving hers. "Katie Donovan, will you do me the honor of becoming my wife as soon as we get to Oregon and a church? Will you allow me to be a father to your younger brother and sister?"

"Oh, yes, Jason, I will." Katie bounced on her toes. When Jason didn't stand quickly enough, she bent forward and met his upturned lips in a sweet kiss.

He stood and nodded beyond her. "Do I need to ask him, too?"

Katie peered over her shoulder. Tommy and Rachel stood not more than twenty feet away watching and listening to every word that was said. She laughed. "Tommy, Jason wants to know if he can marry me. Do you care? He's willing to take on the job of raising the kids, too."

Rachel squealed her approval as she ran the short distance to grab Katie in a hug.

Tommy grinned and shook his head. "No problem. You've got my permission and blessing."

Tommy and Jason shook hands and clapped each other on the back while Rachel and Katie laughed and hugged again.

Jason slipped his arm around Katie and drew her to his side for another kiss right in front of the other two.

While warmth crept from her heart to her face, Katie absorbed his love. Although he hadn't used the words, he'd shown his heart, and that would have to be enough.

Then he pulled away barely enough to rest his forehead against hers while he spoke low for her ears alone. "Katie, I love you more than my own life. I didn't know how I would get through each day without you. Our life may not be easy, but our love will sustain us and make the rough places smooth. I will always love you, sweetheart."

Tears sprang to her eyes as a smile lifted the corners of her lips. Now he used the right words. "Oh, Jason—"

She didn't finish as he again covered her lips with his. Her heart pounded out the rhythm of love while joy filled her heart. Mama was right. God had chosen someone special for her, and she'd almost ruined God's best by trying to figure things out and get ahead of His timing. *Thank you, Father, for working everything out for good in spite of my foolish interference. Help us walk together with You in our new home. Let our love grow and see us through whatever lies ahead. Amen.*

About the Author

Mildred Colvin is an award-winning author of seventeen romance novels in both historical and contemporary themes, two compilations, and one audio book.

Mildred is a member of American Christian Fiction Writers and is active in two critique groups. To keep up with her writing and activities, visit her at Romantic Reflections http://mildredcolvin.blogspot.com and Infinite Characters http://infinitecharacters.com

The Oregon Trail conclusion coming soon!

Home's Promise

Continue the story of Katie Donovan and Rachel Morgan as they settle into their new homes in Oregon. Tommy finally asks Rachel to marry him, but God has placed a call to the ministry on his heart. Rachel doesn't mind waiting a couple of months for her wedding until she begins to wonder if Tommy is taking her for granted. When a new neighbor shows interest in Rachel, she isn't sure what to do, and Tommy's admiration for a girl back in town doesn't help matters. Will their love survive the pressures of being apart after so much time spent together on the trail? Or will they be led in new directions?

Available now in E-book and Paperback:

Learning to Lean
A New Life
Love Returned
Cora's Deception
Eliza's Mistake
This Child Is Mine

In E-book:
Lesson of the Poinsettia

You might also like:

By Regina Tittel
www.etsy.com
The Ozark Durham Series
Abandoned Hearts—Book One
Unexpected Kiss—Book Two
Coveted Bride—Book Three

Coming Fall 2012
From White Rose Publishing, Pelican Books
http://www.pelicanbookgroup.com
Madeline's Protector
By Vanessa Riley
~*~*~*~

Made in the USA
Lexington, KY
14 December 2012